The Secret of
Tabby Mountain

The Jo Barkley Series

The Secret of
Tabby Mountain

Neva Andrews

Writers Club Press
San Jose New York Lincoln Shanghai

The Secret of Tabby Mountain

Writers Club Press
an imprint of iUniverse.com, Inc.

For information address:
iUniverse.com, Inc.
5220 S 16th, Ste. 200
Lincoln, NE 68512
www.iuniverse.com

Cover art by Kim Andrews

ISBN: 0-595-19362-5

Printed in the United States of America

To Ed,
whose love
allows me to pursue my dream.

Acknowledgements

Research is an interesting part of writing fiction set in a real place and time period. On our way back from a visit in southern Idaho, Ed and I took a side trip through Heber, Strawberry Valley, Tabiona, and Vernal, Utah. My interest in Chief Tabby was sparked by a plaque erected by the Daughters of Pioneers in 1939 on the grounds of Wasatch County Court House in Heber, Utah. Further research confirmed their report that Bishop Murdock had invited Chief Tabby to his home for a barbeque in 1867, and the chief signed a treaty that ended the Indian attacks on the settlements in that valley.

Originally, Uncle Clint's ranch was to be in Strawberry Valley, Utah. At the Visitors Center in Heber, I was told there are no ranches in Strawberry Valley and never have been. This was confirmed at the Strawberry Visitors Center. I had done enough research to know of a little town called Tabiona. As we crossed the Duchesne River, and Tabiona Valley lay before us, I knew this was the setting for Uncle Clint's ranch. We spent an interesting hour visiting with Leo Turnbow and his wife at their 80 acre ranch adjacent to the Ouwray-Ute Reservation. They were very helpful and gave us a feel for the local area. It was there I learned of the potguts squirrel. They also introduced us to an interesting booklet, *Foot Prints in a Beautiful Valley*, compiled and published by Tabiona & Hanna Communities, and not available commercially.

To supplement my own observations of the flora and fauna of the area, I read books and pamphlets. Among the most helpful were, *The Southern Rockies, Colorado, Utah* from The Smithsonian Guides to Natural America; and Betty McCarthy's, *America the Beautiful. Utah.*

For background on Ute history, I read several books. The most helpful were, *The World of Wakara*, by Conway Sonne; and *Utah's Black Hawk War*, by Carlton Culmsee. I also gleaned information from the history page of the Official Website of the Northern Ute Tribe. When I needed more information about Chief Tabby, Gloria Mtn. Lion of the Ute Tribe Cultural Rights and Protection at Ft. Duchesne was most helpful as was Doris Burton, historian at Uinta County Library in Vernal, Utah. Some sources had Wakara as Tabby's older brother, others as his uncle.

Thanks to my husband, Ed, for his patience in manuscript preparation; to son, Bill, for data entry; and to daughter-in-law, Kim, for the cover art. Thanks to the staff at Adams County Library who continue to encourage me and help with research. Special thanks to my editor, Eileen Gornall, who worked with me to improve the manuscript, and Karen Lemke who did her usual careful job of proofreading. I shall be eternally grateful for my critique group who encourage me and don't let me get away with sloppy writing, and for my prayer partners who cheer me on.

One

On May 16, 1935, Jo Barkley burst into the kitchen waving an envelope in her hand.

"Hey, Mom, a letter from Uncle Clint. Can I open it?"

A short, sturdy woman turned from the worktable where she was rolling out bread dough to make cinnamon rolls. A full length apron protected her print dress. Her black hair lay in neat waves back from her face and worry lines showed between her eyebrows.

"Is it addressed to Miss Josephine Barkley?"

"No. It's addressed to Mr. and Mrs. Frank Barkley, Rural Route 3, Delta, Utah."

"Then lay it on the table," Mom said. "I'll look at it when I get the cinnamon rolls made and the bread in the pans. You may get the fire going for me."

Jo laid the letter on the round kitchen table and ran her fingers through her copper colored curls. How could Mom be so calm about a letter from Uncle Clint?

Maybe he needed help on the ranch. She went to the wood cookstove in the corner and lifted the lid. As she scraped down the ashes and laid crumpled paper and kindling in the firebox, she pictured herself riding a real cow pony on Uncle Clint's ranch. Her hands trembled with excitement as she took a match from the box in the warming oven and lit the fire.

The tangy smell of burning cedar bark filled the room as Mom put the last perfectly shaped loaf of bread in the pan and covered the loaves and cinnamon rolls with a clean, flour-sack dish towel. She washed her hands at the washstand on the porch and threw the water out the back door. Then she carefully dried them on the towel at the end of the worktable before picking up the letter.

Jo stuffed her hands in the pockets of her bib overalls. She wanted to grab the letter and tear it open. She felt a thousand grasshoppers jumping in her stomach. Mom took a paring knife from the drawer and slit the envelope along the top edge.

"Oh, my goodness." The worry lines on her forehead deepened as she read the letter.

"What does he say, Mom?" Jo hopped up and down on one bare foot.

"He wants you and Bobby to come to the ranch next month to help with the spring cattle drive."

"Oh, can we Mom? Can we?" Jo wanted to turn cartwheels right there in the kitchen.

"We've invited Flora Mae, remember? She'll arrive day after tomorrow to spend the rest of the summer with you. After being so sick during the winter, I don't think she'd be strong enough to go to the ranch."

"Darn that Flora Mae! Why does she have to come anyway? She's—"

"Josephine Sue Barkley, watch your tongue. That's no way to talk about your cousin."

Jo ran outside. She slammed the screen door behind her. The grasshoppers in her stomach turned to stinging ants. She kicked a tin can and ignored the complaint from her bare toes. On she ran, past the pump and the woodpile, through the corral, past the cattail bog, and down the dusty cow trail to the pasture.

At the willow patch, Jo threw herself down in the salt grass and let the tears flow. She wrestled with thoughts of Flora Mae, thoughts too horrible to put into words. Tippy came and licked her face. She sat up and put her arm around the dog's neck.

"Oh, Tippy, why does that sissy Flora Mae have to come, anyway? You know what a pantywaist she was last summer." Jo remembered the Fourth-of-July when Flora Mae was afraid to set off a firecracker and couldn't even understand what was fun about riding calves. "If it wasn't for her, Bobby and I could ride in a real cattle drive."

Bobby lived on a farm half a mile south of the Barkley place. He and Jo had shared adventures since they were four. Now at eleven they were old enough to ride in a real cattle drive. This would be the greatest adventure of all.

Jo sat for a long time with Tippy's head in her lap. She scratched him behind his ears and rubbed her face in his soft fur. The zesty smell of willows soothed her mind, and her thoughts turned to Uncle Clint's ranch. She had always wanted to visit the ranch in Tabiona Valley. She'd heard of the beautiful Duchesne River that flowed through the valley and the high Uintah Mountains near by. It would be so different from the farm here on this alkali flat. There were even Indians. Uncle Clint lived near the Ute Indian Reservation.

Jo was determined to have her own spread some day, with white face cattle and lots of good cow ponies. This would be her chance to see how things were done on a real ranch. She had to figure out a way to ride in that cattle drive.

The sun was headed toward the western mountains when Jo finally stood up and spoke to her dog. "Well, Tippy, we may as well take the cows in. The chores have to be done even if the world is falling apart. Go round 'em up, boy." She raised her hand and made a sweeping motion toward the lower pasture. Together they ran to get the cows. "Easy, boy. You know they won't give much milk if we run them."

Tippy quietly headed the cows toward the barn. If one stopped to graze, he nipped her heel and ducked to avoid the wicked jab of her hind foot. Jo walked along behind, so absorbed in her thoughts she didn't notice the stream of fresh manure Pet left in the trail until she stepped in it.

"Yuck!" Jo shuddered as she felt the warm muck squish between her toes. She dragged her bare feet through the grass along the edge of the trail and thought of what Dad had said just the other day. The crops weren't doing well on this alkali flat. Maybe he'd say they couldn't afford a trip to the ranch. She spit at a cow pie. It didn't matter. They couldn't go anyway with Flora Mae coming.

Jo dragged through her chores. She measured the cows' grain into their individual feed boxes and forked hay into the manger in the barn. She imagined what it would be like on Uncle Clint's ranch. They probably had a real barn, with a hay loft and everything, not like this open straw shed.

The rattle of the milk cart interrupted her thoughts. Her brother, Clyde, came with the ten gallon milk can and two buckets. Without a word, Jo took a bucket and grabbed a milk stool. She scuffed her toes in the loose dirt of the barn floor as she stepped to her favorite cow. Jo pressed her head into the cow's flank and felt Pet's warm belly against her shoulder. She listened to the rasp of rough tongues in the wooden feed boxes. The milk beat a rapid rhythm in the bottom of the empty bucket and soon foam began to rise. But thoughts still blew like tumbleweeds through her mind.

"What's the matter, Sis?" Clyde pulled his stool up to the cow on the other side of Pet. "You're sure quiet tonight."

Clyde was four years older than Jo. He loved to tease, but he could be a good friend, too.

"Didn't Mom tell you about the letter from Uncle Clint?"

"No. She wasn't in the house when I came in. Guess she must be out in the garden. What about the letter?"

"He wants Bobby and me to come help with the spring cattle drive."

"Great! That should make you happy."

"Yeah, but Flora Mae's comin'."

"Oh, yeah, I forgot. She got over her sick spell, didn't she?"

"Yes, but the folks thought a summer on the farm would make her stronger. Of course, I have to be her nursemaid!" Jo gave one last furious pull on Pet's teat and got up to empty her bucket into the strainer in the ten gallon milk can. They finished the milking in silence.

Clyde lifted the ten gallon milk can onto the cart as if it were filled with feathers. Jo watched him with pride. He was average height and only weighed 120 pounds, but it was all muscle.

"Gee, Sis, I'm sorry you can't go to the ranch," he said as they started toward the house, "but I don't know what we can do about it. The folks already promised Flora Mae she could come."

"I know."

Dad came up from the pigpen, swinging the slop bucket in his big right hand. His long strides reminded Jo of when she used to try to walk in his footsteps. His straw hat was pushed back on his head, revealing a strip of fair skin above his deeply tanned face. He wore blue bib overalls tucked into laced boots.

In a few minutes, the family of four gathered around the kitchen table and bowed their heads while Dad said the blessing. Even the smell of fresh cinnamon rolls couldn't lift the gloom from Jo's mind. While they ate, Mom told about Uncle Clint's letter and his request for help with the cattle drive.

"What do you say, Jo? Think you'd like to spend a couple weeks on your uncle's ranch?" Dad's sky blue eyes twinkled as he looked across the table at his daughter.

Jo glared at her bowl of bread and milk. "Flora Mae's comin'," she said, without looking up.

"Oh, that's right. I'm sorry, Jo. That would be great fun for you and Bobby. Good experience, too, but I s'pose there'll be another time."

Jo gritted her teeth. Didn't Dad care she was going to miss the opportunity of her life?

"May I be excused?" she asked. "I'm goin' for a ride on Prince."

"What about the woodbox?" Mom looked across the table at her daughter.

"Oh, yeah. I forgot. Can I go after I get the wood and kindlin'?"

"Just be back by bedtime," Dad said.

Jo picked up the kindling box and went out the door. The sun had already dropped behind the distant mountains. At the woodpile, she sat on a log and nibbled a cedar chip. The bitter taste fit her mood. Even in her despair, though, Jo felt the magic of the evening. A small gray cloud edged in rose hung near the western horizon. She watched the nighthawks swoop to catch their evening meal, heard the burrowing owl call "cu-coo."

As the light in the western sky faded, the mountains turned purple and the evening star appeared. Jo whispered:

"Star light, star bright,
First star I see tonight,
I wish I may, I wish I might
Have the wish I wish tonight."

Tippy barked. Bobby's dog, Shepp, came bounding up the driveway, and Jo turned to see Bobby ride into the yard on his horse, Flaxen. Bare feet dangled below bib overalls and his blond hair looked like his mother put a bowl on his head and cut around the edges.

"Hi, short stuff. What brings you out tonight?" Jo threw down the cedar chip she'd been nibbling.

"Aren't your chores done yet? I wanna go for a ride."

"Get off that long legged horse of yours and help me get this wood in. Then we'll go for a ride. We need to talk."

"What've I done now?"

"Nothin'. We just need to talk."

When the woodbox was full, Jo caught Prince and she and Bobby rode down the winding driveway. Tall greasewood bushes, with their green, needle-like leaves and sharp thorns grew close on either side. At the road, they turned south across the bridge then swung west along a dirt road that followed the canal. The damp smell hung heavy on the evening air. Greasewood grew here and there in the wasteland to their left. They rode in silence for a while, Bobby on his tall sorrel gelding, Jo on her short Welsh pony. Shepp and Tippy romped along, taking side trips to check out fresh scents.

Bobby finally broke the silence. "Well, what did you want to talk about?"

"Uncle Clint wants us to come to the ranch to help with the spring cattle drive."

"Hot ziggity dog! I'll ask my folks. I'm sure they'll let me go. When do we leave?"

"We don't. That's the problem."

"How come?" Bobby turned and scowled at Jo.

"Flora Mae's comin' for the summer. Remember what a pantywaist she was last summer?"

"I thought she was kinda nice."

"Wipe that silly grin off your face. She was a real pain. She had a sick spell last winter and my folks thought a summer on the farm would help her get strong again. I think Mom hopes some of her 'lady-like' ways will rub off on me. Anyway, I been appointed nursemaid."

Neither said anything for a while. Then Bobby asked, "How soon does your Uncle Clint want us?"

"About three weeks."

"I've got an idea. In three weeks, with good farm food and plenty of fresh air and exercise, she'll be strong enough to go to the ranch with us."

"Bobby, you crazy? Take Flora Mae to the ranch? She'd ruin everything."

A nearly full moon had risen behind them and the greasewood cast eerie shadows along the trail.

"We better head back," Jo said. "I'll be in trouble with Dad if I'm not home by bedtime."

Jo lay awake far into the night thinking about Bobby's suggestion. Would it be any fun at the ranch with Flora Mae? Would she even want to go? What would Flora Mae's folks say? What about Mom and Dad? Would they agree to it? Maybe it would be better to stay home. Flora Mae would be such a drag.

Jo pulled her pillow over her head and fell into a fitful sleep. She dreamed they were at the ranch. She, Bobby, and Flora Mae were exploring a cave, and Flora Mae turned into a huge snake. Just as it was about to strangle Jo, Bobby whipped out his sword and killed the snake. Jo woke up with a start. She felt clammy all over. Her pillow was wet with sweat. She puzzled over the dream for a long time. Tomorrow she'd have to talk to Grandpa. Finally, her mind quieted enough to go back to sleep.

Two

After chores were done the next evening, Jo jumped on Prince and rode over to Grandpa's. She found him out by the corral trimming the hooves on one of his work horses.

Jo thought how strong he looked as he held Old Ned's hoof in his big left hand. Dirt stained his striped bib overalls and a breeze ruffled his gray hair. His straw hat lay on a bench by the barn.

Jo slid off Prince and tied him to the wagon.

"Well, if it isn't my Punkin. What brings you over here at this late hour?" Grandpa dropped the hoof he was working on and turned to smile at Jo. His clear blue eyes sparkled and smile-lines creased his leathery face.

"I gotta talk to you, Grandpa."

"Well, hold on till I get this hoof finished. It's the last one for today."

Jo watched as Grandpa trimmed Old Ned's hoof with the hoof nippers. They looked like the pincers Dad used to cut rivets.

"Here, Punkin, take these nippers and hand me the hoof knife."

"How do you know how much to cut away?" Jo asked as she handed Grandpa the knife.

"Well, how do you know how much of your toe nail to trim?" Grandpa said. "It's not too much different. You trim off what's in his way. See this part?" Grandpa pointed to the soft area in the center of the horse's foot. "That's the frog. You have to be careful not to trim too close to that. He'd have a sore foot just like you'd have a sore toe if you trimmed your toe nail too short."

"Grandpa, how did you learn so much about horses?"

"Working with them all my life, I guess. I'll just smooth this up a little with that rasp and I'll be through." Grandpa turned Old Ned into the corral and gave him a loving pat on the rump.

"Now, what's bothering you, Punkin?" They sat on the bench by the barn.

"Does God speak to people in dreams?" Jo asked.

"He did back in Bible times. I think it's very rare today. You see, we have the Bible to tell us about God."

"But what if God did speak to you in a dream? How would you know?"

"I'd compare my dream with what God says in the Bible. What did you dream, Punkin?"

Jo told Grandpa about Uncle Clint's letter and Bobby's suggestion that Flora Mae go to the ranch with them. Then she told him her dream.

"I was scared, Grandpa. I thought God was telling me that something awful will happen if Flora Mae goes to the ranch."

"Sometimes we play out our anxieties in our dreams. This doesn't sound like God speaking. Why are you worried about Flora Mae going to the ranch?"

"Oh, Grandpa, she's such a scaredy-cat. I think she'd ruin all our fun."

"How do you think you'd feel in the city, Punkin? Everything would be so strange. Don't you think you'd be a little bit afraid?"

"Probably." Jo scuffed her big toe in the loose dirt. "I never thought of that."

They sat for a while and listened to the horses and cows munching their evening feed. A horse blew the dust from his nose. The sparrows chattered as they fought over their roosting places. A nighthawk swooped and darted in search of his evening meal. Jo heard a coyote yipping in the distance. Even the familiar smell of dry hay and manure seemed to quiet her mind.

Finally, she said, "If I help her get used to things on the farm, maybe she won't be such a fraidy-cat. Do you think I could ever learn to like Flora Mae?"

"It might be worth a try. Now you'd better get on home before your folks get worried about you."

"Thanks, Grandpa." Jo gave him a hug and jumped on Prince. In the gathering dusk, they loped out the gate and down the road toward home.

Uncle Charlie, Aunt Bessie, and Flora Mae arrived about noon the next day. Jo took one look at Flora Mae's pale face framed in black Shirley Temple curls. The image of the breakable China doll in the store window flashed through her mind as it had last summer when Flora Mae came for a visit. Only now, she looked even more fragile in her yellow voile dress.

Jo forced a smile and invited Flora Mae to join her in the kitchen while she finished setting the table. Grandpa and Grandma came for dinner. It wasn't even Sunday and they had a real company dinner, fried chicken, mashed potatoes and everything. Mom had made a cake and Grandma brought lemon meringue pie. After Grandpa said the blessing, Jo listened as the grown-ups talked about the weather, the crops, and President Roosevelt's latest idea for ending the Depression. How could they talk about these boring things? Wasn't anyone going to mention Uncle Clint's letter? Finally, Grandpa changed the subject.

"I hear Clint wants some help with the spring cattle drive next month."

"Yes. We got a letter the other day asking if Jo and Bobby could come. But, of course, Jo already had other plans." Dad smiled at Flora Mae.

"Can Flora Mae come to the ranch with us, Aunt Bessie?" Jo blurted. Then she caught Mom's look of disapproval. "I mean, please, Aunt

Bessie, may Flora Mae come with us? The mountain air would be good for her."

"Is it a real ranch up in the mountains? That sounds romantic! I'd love to go!" Flora Mae had been eating quietly and listening to the adult conversation. Now she laid her fork on her plate. She looked at her mother as if she were used to getting her own way by coaxing. "Oh, may I Mother?"

"I don't know." Aunt Bessie wrinkled her brow. "Maybe Clint and Myrtle wouldn't have time to look after a frail young lady like you."

"It's three weeks yet," Jo said. "Flora Mae'll be stronger by then with all the fresh air and sunshine and good food here on the farm."

"I'm sure Clint and Myrtle would be happy to have her," Grandpa said. "Myrtle specializes in nursing young ones back to health whether it's an injured bird, or an orphaned calf, or a young lady like Flora Mae."

"Well," Dad said, "she'd have to learn how to be useful on a ranch. Jo, do you think you can teach Flora Mae to ride a horse and do chores?"

"Sure," Jo said. "In three weeks you can learn to ride a horse and milk a cow, can't you Flora Mae?"

"I don't know if I can, but I'll try if you'll teach me."

"Are you sure, dear, you want to do this? I don't know if you're strong enough yet." Aunt Bessie looked lovingly at her daughter.

"Yes, Mother, I want to try. Jo will help me, won't you Jo?"

"Sure. We'll start with easy chores first. You'll do fine." Jo wished she felt as confident as she sounded.

"Well, I guess." Aunt Bessie turned to her sister. "You and Frank will have to decide if she's strong enough to go when the time comes."

"We'll keep an eye on her," Dad said. " First thing you know, she'll be a regular farm hand."

The next morning after breakfast, the girls headed for the hen house. Flora Mae carried a small, empty lard bucket and Jo, a coffee can with grain for the chickens. She thought gathering the eggs would be the easiest chore to teach Flora Mae, but she forgot about the old red hen who was trying to set.

Jo opened the gate to the chicken yard and scattered the grain on the ground. Flora Mae followed her into the pen, tip-toeing to avoid the chicken manure. When Jo opened the door to the hen house, chickens came out squawking and flapping their wings. Flora Mae squealed and covered her face with her hands.

"They won't hurt you," Jo said. "They'll scratch around out here while we go in the hen house and gather the eggs."

In the dim interior, the girls saw several nest boxes with eggs in them. They gathered the eggs and put them in the lard bucket. On one nest sat an old red hen. She ruffled her feathers and clucked a warning as Jo approached.

"This one thinks she's going to be a mother," Jo said, "but Mom doesn't want her setting right now. We need the eggs."

"How are we going to get her eggs?" Flora Mae asked.

"I'll get hold of her neck so she can't peck you and you reach under and get the eggs." As Jo moved closer, the hen lashed out wickedly with her beak. "Take it easy biddy."

Jo made a quick grab for the hen's neck but missed. The hen flew off the nest, bounced off Flora Mae's face, and ran cackling into the chicken yard. With a screech, Flora Mae dropped the bucket of eggs. Jo lunged to save the eggs but lost her footing in the chicken manure and landed on her face in a pile of broken eggs. She sat up. As she began wiping slimy egg off her face, Flora Mae dissolved into uncontrollable giggles. Angry words flashed through Jo's mind. Then, realizing how ridiculous she must look, she, too, began to giggle.

"Ish," Flora Mae said. "Jo, you're a sight. I couldn't help laughing."

"I'm washable," Jo said, "but we won't have eggs for breakfast for a while. Come on. After we get the mess cleaned up, I'll come back and gather the rest of the eggs."

Later that day, Jo moved the old red hen into a small pen away from the other chickens. Jo could hardly believe it, but Flora Mae kept practicing and soon she could feed the chickens and gather the eggs by herself. On the morning of the fourth day, Jo decided it was time to help Flora Mae get over some of her fears.

"C'mon, Flora Mae, let's go swing on the derrick." Jo tugged on her cousin's hand. Flora Mae pulled her hand away.

"What's the derrick?"

"It's the hay stacker. It's made of poles and has cables and pulleys to pull loads of loose hay up onto the stack. We've got the cable fastened so the pulleys hang above the stack and we can swing from them."

"I don't feel like it. Why don't we play paper dolls? I'll let you play with my Shirley Temple doll."

"We can play paper dolls tonight. C'mon. I'll show you. Bobby'll think you're spunky."

Flora Mae's eyes lit up. "Will Bobby be there? I remember him from last summer. He's cute."

"He's coming later this morning. I'll teach you before he gets here. You just grab the pulleys and jump off the haystack. It's great fun."

"Doesn't it hurt when you hit the ground?" Flora Mae's face turned a shade whiter.

"You don't hit the ground. Well, you don't exactly jump off, you run off the stack and swing out over nothin' and the cable brings you back again."

"Isn't it scary?"

"Naw. Not very."

"Well, maybe I'll try." Flora Mae followed Jo out the door. As they joined hands to run across the yard, Jo felt Flora Mae's hand tremble.

"C'mon. Don't be scared. It'll be fun once you get used to it."

At the haystack, Jo scrambled up the ladder. Flora Mae stood at the bottom and looked up at Jo.

"Come on up," Jo called.

"I can't. I'm scared. It's too high." Flora Mae's voice was barely above a whisper.

Jo climbed back down.

"You go up. I'll be right behind you. There's no way you can fall."

Carefully, Flora Mae climbed, one rung at a time. At last, they made it to the top.

"Now that wasn't so bad, was it?" Jo asked. Flora Mae's face was chalky against her black hair. She crumpled onto the hay and lay there whimpering.

"I can't get back down," she whispered.

"Sure you can. After we swing awhile, you just climb back down the ladder."

"I can't."

Suddenly, Jo got worried. Flora Mae was trembling. Her face was as white as the alkali down by the cattail bog. Maybe she couldn't climb back down the ladder as scared as she was. What should they do? They could just sit up here until Dad came in from the field, but then they'd be in real trouble. Dad might even say they couldn't go to the ranch. Jo plopped down in the dusty hay and tried to think what to do.

"Hallo— Where are you?" a cheerful voice called from behind the haystack.

"Up here, Bobby. Boy, am I glad to see you. Come on up. We got a problem."

Three

Bobby climbed the ladder and crawled onto the stack. Flora Mae sat out in the middle, hugging her knees and whimpering.

"What's the matter with her?"

"She's scared spitless. Won't listen to reason."

"What did you do to her?"

"Nothin'. Just helped her climb up the ladder. Now she won't swing and she won't climb down."

"Hey, you do have a problem."

"*We* have a problem. Bobby, you've got to help me. If Dad finds us up here with her scared like that, he won't let us go to the ranch."

"O.K., so what do we do?"

"If you go down and untie the cable and wrap it around a derrick pole, do you think you could hold on tight enough to ease the pulleys down with one of us on them?"

"I don't know. Maybe we better put a harness on Marybel and hitch her to the cable."

"We don't have time. It's almost dinner time and Dad will be in from the field. I'll ride down first to try it out."

"So, you think it's better you get killed than Flora Mae?"

"Nobody's gonna get killed. Maybe busted up a little. I'll come down and help you untie the cable. First let's throw hay down to make a pile to land on in case it doesn't work." Jo turned to Flora Mae. "I'll be right back. You sit here and try to relax. Don't worry, we'll get you down."

Jo and Bobby threw some hay off the stack then climbed down the ladder.

Jo pushed the hay into a pile. "There, that should do it. Now if we can just get that cable untied." They untied the cable and made a wrap around the pole.

"I should be able to hold it," Bobby said as he took hold of the cable with his bare hands.

Jo went back up on the stack and made a loop in the rope that hung from the pulleys. She tied it securely, leaving a length of rope hanging.

"O.K., Flora Mae, now watch me."

Jo slipped one leg through the loop in the rope and hung onto the pulleys with both hands. Then she went to the edge of the haystack.

"Ready?" she called down to Bobby.

"Ready."

"Here I come." Jo pushed off with her feet and swung out from the stack, gliding safely to the pile of loose hay. While she climbed the ladder, Bobby pulled on the cable to bring the pulleys up to the stack again.

"Now it's your turn," Jo said.

"I can't." Flora Mae reminded Jo of a kitten that had climbed a tree and couldn't get down.

"Sure you can. There's nothin' to it. Just sit in the rope sling and Bobby will ease you down."

"You go down with me."

"Can't do that. Bobby couldn't hold both of us. We'd crash."

Jo continued to coax Flora Mae until finally she put her leg through the loop and took hold of the pulleys.

"Now wait till I get down below."

"Hurry. I'm getting scared again."

"Just hang on to the pulleys." Jo hurried back down the ladder. "You ready, Bobby?"

"Ready."

"O.K., Flora Mae, push off."

"I can't."

"Well, sit down on the edge of the stack, then, and throw me the end of the rope. Now hang on."

Jo grasped the rope as it came down. She pulled Flora Mae away from the stack. Flora Mae let out a screech and glided safely to the pile of hay. She was shaking all over as Jo helped her up and brushed the hay from her clothes.

"I've never been so scared in my life." Flora Mae's voice trembled. "I'll never do that again."

"I'm just glad we got you down safe and sound," Jo said.

Jo noticed Bobby's hands. They were raw from handling the rough cable.

"We better go in the house and take care those hands."

"Naw, your mom would worry about me. I'll go home and fix them up."

Soon Dad came in from the field and the family gathered around the table in the kitchen for the noon meal. After the blessing, Dad asked Flora Mae if they'd found anything interesting to do during the morning.

"We played on the haystack," Jo said before Flora Mae had a chance to answer.

"Did anybody get hurt?" Clyde asked.

"Bobby hurt his hands. They looked awful," Flora Mae said.

"Oh, they're just roughed up a little." Jo felt trapped. She shot a look at Flora Mae.

"Jo, you look like a cornered coyote. What were you up to this time?" Dad eyed her with his half-amused, half-stern look. Was she in trouble?

"Flora Mae and I climbed up on the haystack. We were going to swing on the pulleys—"

"Frank, don't you think that's too dangerous for the girls?" Mom had those deep worry lines between her eyes again.

"Now, Mama, don't worry. It's not dangerous if they use their heads and do it right. Now tell us what happened, Jo."

"Flora Mae got scared. She wouldn't swing and she wouldn't climb back down the ladder."

"Oh, Uncle Frank, I tried, but I was so frightened I couldn't move." Tears glistened in Flora Mae's eyes.

"There, now, don't cry. You don't have to swing from the derrick to be a good farmhand." Dad turned to Jo. "How did you get her down?"

Jo explained the rescue. She made sure to tell about the pile of loose hay to land on, and that she went down first to try it out.

"Well, you used your head after all. I'm not surprised Bobby's hands are sore. Those cables can be awful rough on bare hands."

"What hair-brained idea do you have cooked up next, Jo?" Clyde's eyes twinkled and his lips held the hint of a grin. Jo ignored the dig.

"I thought Flora Mae might like to rest this afternoon. Then tomorrow we can start riding lessons if you're up to it, Flora Mae."

"May I ride in a saddle?"

"Sorry, we don't have a saddle," Jo said.

"It's better to learn bareback, anyway," Dad said. "That way you learn to go with your horse, and it's safer." Dad always said that, but Jo didn't always go with her horse. She got dumped lots of times.

"I'll try," Flora Mae said. "Marybel isn't as high as a haystack."

Clyde laughed. "No, and she doesn't move much faster." Jo made a face at Clyde.

"While you're riding, you can herd the cows," Dad said.

"What do you mean by herd the cows, Uncle Frank? I thought the cows were all right by themselves in the pasture during the day."

"The pasture's getting short and there's lots of good grass out along the canal. Jo takes them out and watches them while they graze."

"Oh." Flora Mae turned to Jo. "And you ride while you're doing this?"

"Yes. You can ride Marybel and I'll ride Prince."

When the chores were done that evening, Flora Mae got out her Shirley Temple paper dolls.

"Do we have to play paper dolls?" Jo hadn't played paper dolls since she was eight years old.

"You promised."

"Okay, how do we play?" Jo followed Flora Mae to the porch.

"We'll have them act out the latest Shirley Temple movie."

"I haven't seen any Shirley Temple movies."

"I'll tell you what to do and what your lines are."

Jo's mind kept drifting back to the haystack. She couldn't figure out why Flora Mae got so scared. When it was her turn, she couldn't remember what to say.

"You're not paying attention," Flora Mae said. "I might as well play by myself. I have to do both parts anyway."

"Sorry, I just can't seem to get the hang of it. Why don't we play marbles instead?"

"You go play marbles if you want. I'm going to play with my Shirley Temple dolls."

Jo left Flora Mae with her paper dolls and went out to find Tippy. She wondered if she'd ever learn to get along with her cousin.

The next few days went well without any disasters. Jo noticed that Flora Mae seemed stronger each day. Maybe she *could* adjust to farm life. Soon she was able to ride Marybel on the walk and slow trot. Jo decided it was time to teach her to ride at a gallop.

A patch of wasteland lay south of the Barkley place. A large area in the center was white and hard like concrete. Greasewood grew in the sandy soil surrounding the hardpan. It seemed to Jo the ideal place to teach her riding student to stay with her horse at a gallop.

"We'll go out to the hardpan," Jo said. "There's a sandy area out there where it won't hurt so much if you fall off."

"Fall off?" Flora Mae gasped. "I don't want to fall off. Maybe we shouldn't—"

"You can't ride the rest of your life at a walk!" Jo snapped, then softened her tone. "If we're going to Uncle Clint's ranch, you've got to learn to ride a horse at a gallop."

Without waiting for an answer, Jo headed for the hardpan on Prince. Flora Mae followed on Marybel.

When they came to the sandy place, Jo said, "Lift the reins and give her a kick in the side. Then hang on with your legs. Like this." She urged Prince to a gallop. Jo rode a little way ahead, then circled back to see how Flora Mae was doing and to ride along beside her. Flora Mae was hunched over, clinging to Marybel's mane. She didn't look very relaxed, but she was staying on top.

"That's good," Jo said. "Now just relax and enjoy the ride."

Before Flora Mae could answer, Jo shouted, "Watch out! There's a badger hole."

Flora Mae screamed and went flying. She landed in the soft dirt a few feet ahead of her mount. Marybel squealed, toppled forward, and fell on her right side. Jo slid off Prince and ran to her.

"Easy, girl." Jo rubbed her neck and patted her as Marybel thrashed around trying to get on her feet. Gradually she relaxed under Jo's gentle hands and soothing voice, and Jo was able to examine the injured leg. Her stomach churned as she saw a jagged bone protruding from the skin half way between the knee and the hoof. "I'm sorry girl. You'll never run again."

Jo looked up to see Flora Mae dusting the dirt off her bib overalls. "Are you all right?"

"I think so. Marybel's hurt real bad, isn't she?"

"You've got to get on Prince and go get Dad."

"I can't. I'm never getting on another horse."

"You've got to. I can't leave Marybel and she needs Dad."

Jo caught Prince and boosted Flora Mae on.

"I can't go fast. I'll fall off again."

"Just go," Jo said. "And tell Dad to bring his rifle."

Four

Jo went behind a greasewood and threw up. Then she went back to Marybel, sat on the ground, and buried her face in Marybel's mane. Her body shook with silent sobs.

"I'm sorry, old girl," Jo said. "I can't bear the thought of Dad shooting you, but I know it's the only way. You'll never use that leg again. The sooner we put you out of your misery the better off you'll be. I'll miss you. You've been a wonderful pal. I've never stopped loving you, even when Prince came into my life. There'll never be another Marybel."

Jo sat there in the warm May sunshine and shivered as if in a winter blizzard. When Marybel tried to struggle to her feet, Jo stroked her neck and calmed her with quiet words. Marybel lay back trembling and nickered as if to say, "Thank you for staying with me, Jo."

Dad rode up at a gallop. He slid off Prince and stood his rifle against a greasewood. Then he knelt beside Jo and put his arm around her shoulder.

"I'm sorry, Jo," he said. "That leg looks really bad. We'll have to shoot her."

"I know," Jo said. "Just let me get away first." She ran to Prince, jumped on and kicked him to a wild run. "I don't care where you take me," she said. "Just get me away from here."

How long they raced along the dirt road, Jo didn't know. Her mind was numb. All feeling had gone out of her. Only an emptiness remained. Gradually her mind cleared and she realized she had guided Prince to Grandpa's place. They turned in at the gate and he met them in front of the house. He helped her from the pony and gathered her in his arms. She leaned against his chest, her body racked with silent sobs.

"What's the matter, Punkin? Can you tell me about it?"

"Oh, Grandpa, it was awful." Jo swiped her sleeve across her eyes. Grandpa pulled a bandana from his hip pocket and she blew her nose. As they sat on a bench by the back door, Jo explained.

"We were in the greasewood out by the hardpan. I was teaching Flora Mae to ride at a gallop. Marybel stepped in a badger hole and broke her leg. Dad had to shoot her."

Grandpa drew her close. Neither spoke for a time. She nestled in the comfort of his strong right arm and knew he felt her pain.

Finally Jo said, "If Flora Mae hadn't come, this wouldn't have happened."

Grandpa remained silent for a while. Then in his quiet way he said, "Blaming Flora Mae won't ease the pain."

"I know. It was my fault. I knew there were badger holes out there, but I didn't think."

"Blaming yourself won't help, either, Punkin. It was an accident."

"I should have thought about the badger holes, but all I could think of was getting Flora Mae to learn all she needs to know so we can go to Uncle Clint's ranch. Now I've lost Marybel and we won't get to help with the cattle drive."

"I know you're hurting because you've lost Marybel, but why do you think you won't get to go on the cattle drive?"

"Flora Mae won't want to go after what's happened." They sat in silence for several minutes. Then Jo asked, "Grandpa, will there be animals in heaven?"

"Some people think so, but I don't know, Punkin. One thing I do know, if they aren't there, we won't miss them. God tells us in the Bible that he will wipe away all tears from our eyes. Heaven will be a place of complete happiness."

"I don't wanna go to heaven if Marybel isn't there." Jo buried her face in Grandpa's chest and sobbed. Grandpa held her close until she quieted again.

"You're angry with God right now. That's all right. He knows how you're hurting. But what about Flora Mae? She must feel awful. She needs to know you forgive her. Are you big enough for that?"

"I don't know, Grandpa."

As Jo rode home, she thought about what Grandpa had said. She didn't think she could ever forgive Flora Mae.

Later that day, Jo helped dig a hole to bury Marybel. Flora Mae offered to help, but Jo told her to go away. She and Bobby gathered skunk weed to put on the grave. The buttercups were gone already and the cactus hadn't bloomed yet.

Jo was miserable the next two days. Sunday evening Clyde found her and Tippy out by the corral. Jo sat with her back against the haystack and whittled on a willow stick.

"What are you making?" he asked.

"Nothin'."

"May I join you?" He sat down beside her. An occasional trill of a redwing floated up from the cattail bog below the barn. The twittering of the sparrows in the straw shed quieted. The familiar sound of horses and cows chomping their hay soothed Jo's spirit. She could feel Clyde's concern for her.

Finally he broke the silence. "Gee, Sis, you've been about as approachable as a porcupine the last few days. You've hardly even spoken to Flora Mae."

"I know. I can't stand the sight of her. It brings it all back. I see Marybel lying there suffering. Every night when I go to sleep I dream about it."

"I know it's tough, Sis, but you've got to come out of it. In a couple of weeks it'll be time to go to the ranch."

"Flora Mae won't wanna go." Jo threw down the willow stick.

"I think she does want to go. She's been trying real hard to help, even though she's scared of 'most everything."

"Grandpa says I have to forgive her." Jo took a whetstone out of her pocket and began sharpening her knife.

"You know he's right."

"Yeah, I know, but I can't."

All day Monday Jo thought about what Clyde had said. Flora Mae did seem to be trying to help, although Jo thought she was more in the way than anything. Maybe she really did want to go to the ranch. But how could Jo tell her she was sorry?

That evening the girls were out at the woodpile loading the little red wagon with firewood. Suddenly Flora Mae looked up with tears in her eyes and said, "I should have died when I fell from Marybel. Would that make you happy, Jo?"

"Oh, Flora Mae, don't say such an awful thing." A list of sins flashed through Jo's mind. Murder was at the top. It scared her for Flora Mae to talk like that.

"You act like you wish I were dead." Flora Mae choked back a sob. "No matter how hard I try, I can't do anything right."

"Oh, Flora Mae, I'm sorry." Jo put her arm around her cousin. "Guess I haven't been able to see beyond my own hurt."

"Jo, I'm really sorry I caused Marybel to break her leg. I know how much you loved her."

"You didn't make her break her leg. It was an accident. Could've been me riding her."

"Shall we start over?" Flora Mae asked. "Maybe we can learn to get along. I really do want to go to the ranch with you and Bobby."

"Do you, really?"

"Yes, I really do. And I want to learn to do the chores, but it's hard."

"You'll learn." Jo smiled at her cousin and began pulling the wagon load of wood toward the house.

After they finished feeding all the animals the next evening, Jo tried to teach Flora Mae to milk a cow. The cows were in their places munching hay and grain from the manger at the back of the barn. The girls stepped in behind them through the open end of the shed. They could feel the heat from the late afternoon sun as it beat on the straw walls.

"We'll let you learn on Old Jersey," Jo said. "She's the gentlest one. Grab a stool and follow me."

"Where?" Flora Mae asked. "I don't see any stool."

"Here." Jo picked up a one-legged milk stool and handed it to Flora Mae.

"Don't you have a three legged stool? This one will tip over."

"Your feet make the other two legs. It works just fine. Besides, it's easier to nail a couple pieces of two-by-four together into a T like this than to make a three-legged stool."

"Soo, boss," Jo said as she stepped up to Old Jersey and patted her on the rump.

Then she turned to Flora Mae and said, "Now you just sit here on the stool and brush all the loose dirt off her bag. Be sure you don't get any of it in the bucket."

Flora Mae set the bucket out of the way and sat down on the stool.

"You've got to sit closer. You can't even reach all the teats from there."

Flora Mae moved the stool in closer and tried again. She got the bag cleaned off. As she reached for the bucket, the stool tipped and she went sprawling. She got up and brushed the dry manure off her pants, but some of it went in the bucket.

"Here," Jo said, "give me the bucket. While I go rinse it, you practice balancing on the stool."

Jo was back in a jiffy and set the bucket under Old Jersey. Then she knelt beside Flora Mae and showed her how to squeeze the teats to make the milk flow. Flora Mae tried and nothing happened.

"You're squeezing from the bottom up. You've got to squeeze from the top down. Like this." She showed Flora Mae how to curl the tips of her fingers into the palm of her hand starting with the forefinger and going down to the little finger. Flora Mae tried again, and a little stream of milk went into the bucket.

"That's the way," Jo said. "Now all you need is practice."

Jo went to milk one of the other cows. Pretty soon she heard a screech, then a thud and a splash. Jo burst out laughing when she saw Flora Mae sprawled on the barn floor with milk down the front of her overalls and Old Jersey's hind foot in the bucket.

"It's not funny! I hate your old cow! I hate the farm! I want to go home!" Flora Mae burst into tears and ran for the house.

Five

When Jo and Flora Mae went to bed out on the screen porch later that evening, Jo couldn't get to sleep. She lay on her straw mat on the floor and stared at the stars. Flora Mae turned restlessly on the cot nearby.

"Flora Mae, you awake?" Jo whispered.

"Yes. I can't get to sleep."

"I'm sorry I laughed at you out in the barn. I didn't mean to make fun of you."

"Old Jersey switched me with her tail. It startled me so I lost my balance. I must've been a sight." Flora Mae giggled.

"You did look funny sprawled there with your curls all messed up and milk splattered down the front of you." They both erupted into a fit of giggles.

"We better settle down before Dad gets after us."

They were quiet for a little while, then Jo said, "Do you really want to go home?"

"No. I was just mad."

Jo was drifting off to sleep when Flora Mae said, "I feel stronger every day. I think living on your farm is helping."

"Good-night," Jo said. "Tomorrow I'll show you a meadowlark's nest."

Jo and Flora Mae had to herd cows the next day. They rode double on Prince. Flora Mae was riding better every day. When they brought the cows home in the middle of the afternoon, Jo took Flora Mae to see the meadowlark's nest. As they walked through the alfalfa field, a bird flew up practically under their feet.

"Here's the nest," Jo said.

"I can't see it."

"See, it's right there, under that canopy." Sure enough, there was a little hollowed out place in the ground lined with grass with a roof part way over it. Four speckled eggs lay in the nest.

"Dad's going to turn the water into this field tonight. We better build a dam around the nest to protect the meadowlark family."

Jo took out her pocket knife and began to loosen the dirt. Flora Mae helped form a dam all around the nest. Then Jo cut chunks of sod from the ditch bank to reinforce the dam.

"There," she said, "that should keep the water out."

Jo was pleased with the progress Flora Mae made. She could feed the chickens and gather the eggs by herself. She knew how much grain to give each cow and how to give them their hay. Night and morning she milked Old Jersey. One thing Jo couldn't get her to do was climb up on the haystack to pitch down more hay.

One afternoon Bobby rode into the yard on Flaxen. "Hi, you two. What's up?"

"Nothin'," Jo said. "We were just trying to decide what to do this afternoon."

"Let's go over to the old von Hoffman place," Bobby suggested.

"Good idea," Jo said. "I want to check on the kingbirds' nest above the window."

"Where is the von Hoffman place?" Flora Mae asked.

"It's half a mile or so over that way." Jo pointed off to the north east. "It's part of the land Dad farms. We have to herd the cows over there sometimes. Two German brothers used to live there, but the house has been vacant for a long time."

"Oh, that's the place Clyde told me about. I don't think we should play over there," Flora Mae said. "Clyde says the house is haunted."

"Aw, he just likes to tease," Bobby said. "Besides, who's afraid of a haunted house?"

"You can stay here and read your book if you want. Bobby and I are gonna go have some fun."

"I guess I'll come," Flora Mae said.

Jo ran to catch Prince. She jumped on the pony and pulled Flora Mae up behind her. When they got to the von Hoffman place, they tied their horses to what was left of an old corral fence. As Jo turned to look at the house, she felt the prickles on the back of her neck. The spookiness of this place always gave her a feeling of adventure. It reminded her of a ghost town in a western movie she'd seen once. The weathered boards of the old shack were gray as death. Tumble weeds had piled up in the corner where the porch stuck out from the rest of the house. A door sagged on its hinges and a ragged curtain, yellowed with age, flapped through a broken window.

Jo and Bobby started toward the house, but Flora Mae hung back. "I don't think we should play here," she said.

"Aw, come on. We play here all the time." Bobby turned back to encourage Flora Mae.

Jo went to the window where the kingbirds always built their nest. She climbed up on the ledge. By stretching to her full height, she could barely peek into the nest above the window. There were four hungry mouths wide open and squawking for food. The mother kingbird dove at Jo's hair.

"Watch out," Flora Mae squealed, "that mother bird's going to get you."

"Ah, she's all right," Jo said. "She just wants to scare me away from her babies. She thinks I'm gonna to rob her nest. I won't hurt your little ones," she said to the mother bird. Jo jumped to the ground.

"Let's go inside and see what we can find," Bobby suggested.

"Yeah, let's," Jo said. "All the times we've been over here we've never gone inside before."

"I don't think we should," Flora Mae said. "It would be like going in somebody's house without being invited."

"What's the matter? You afraid of ghosts? The ghost of Hans von Hoffman challenges you." Jo made a scary face and raised her hands like she was going to pounce on Flora Mae. Then she laughed.

"Tease me if you want, but I'm not going in there. We shouldn't mess around with other people's things even if they are dead." With a flip of her black curls, Flora Mae turned away. She walked over and sat down on the wooden box that covered the old well.

"You go first," Bobby said.

"What's the matter, you afraid of ghosts, too?"

"No. It's ladies first, you know."

"Sure," Jo scoffed. "When have you ever called me a lady before? Hand me that brick. This window's already broken, but there's still jagged glass around the edges."

Jo took the brick from Bobby and broke out the rest of the glass. Then she climbed through the window and jumped to the floor. A board creaked as she landed. A thick layer of dust covered everything. Jo gagged with the odor of dead mouse and moldy straw.

"Wow, what a mess," Bobby said as he jumped down beside her.

"Yeah, looks like the ghosts aren't very good housekeepers."

Broken glass, rags, socks, a pair of bib overalls, even a pair of long underwear were strewn on the floor.

"Look," Jo said. "The mice have chewed a hole in the old straw mattress."

"What's this?" Bobby picked up a small book from among a pile of old magazines.

"Looks like a Bible." Jo took the book from Bobby. She opened it carefully, afraid it would break in her hands. "I can't read a word of it. Must be some foreign language."

"This place gives me the creeps," Bobby said.

"Yeah," Jo agreed. "Let's get out of here." She went to the door and tried to open it, but it sagged against the floor and wouldn't move. "Guess we'll have to go out the way we came in."

Bobby headed for the window and scrambled out. Jo followed.

"What did you find?" Flora Mae came back to join them by the house.

"No ghosts. Just a Bible."

"Let me see." Flora Mae took the Bible and opened it. "It's in German."

"That figures," Jo said. "The von Hoffman brothers were German, but I didn't know they spoke the language."

"Let's explore down in the old well," Bobby suggested. "Maybe they hid a treasure down there."

"Can't do that. Mom said not to."

"Now who's scared?" Bobby teased. "You're just afraid you can' t climb back out."

"Am not."

"Dare you."

"Flora Mae'll tell."

"Sissy."

Jo's face got hot. She doubled up her fists and took a step toward Bobby. Instead of punching him in the nose, she turned and threw the wooden cover off the well. Forgetting all caution, she jumped to the wooden platform four feet below ground. Jo screamed with pain and crumpled in a heap.

"What's the matter? See a ghost?" Bobby taunted.

"Quit goofing off and get me out of here."

Bobby reached down, grabbed Jo's hand and pulled her out of the well. Blood gushed from Jo's toe.

"Leapin' lizards! That's worse'n a ghost! What happened?"

"I landed on a broken brick. Hurry up and get Flaxen and take me home. I've lost a lot of blood already."

"Oh, Jo—" Flora Mae stood wringing her hands.

"Do you have a clean hankie?" Jo asked.

Flora Mae pulled a handkerchief out of her pocket and handed it to Jo. She folded it into a small square and pressed it against the cut at the base of her big toe.

"Here, hold this while I get a string out of my pocket."

Flora Mae held the hankie in place and Jo tied it to her toe.

"I've got to get home fast, so Bobby's going to take me on Flaxen. You'll have to ride Prince by yourself."

"But I've never ridden him by myself. He'll try to keep up with Flaxen. I can't ride him on a run."

"Leave him tied until we get to the corner. Then get on. He'll walk."

"I can't get on by myself."

"Put him in a ditch. If you can't jump on from there you'll just have to lead him all the way home."

"I'll come back for you," Bobby promised. "Now boost Jo up behind me so I can get her home before she bleeds to death." Blood dripped from the handkerchief.

Six

Mom ran out of the house wiping her hands on her apron as Flaxen skidded to a stop by the back door.

"Jo, you're white as a ghost! What happened?"

"Cut my toe." She tried to sound matter-of-fact so Mom wouldn't worry, but she almost fainted as she slid off the horse. Mom helped her into the house.

"Here," Mom said, "sit in this chair and put your foot up on the white box." The old white box had been in the family longer than Jo. It held clean rags and also served as an extra seat at the table when there weren't enough chairs.

Mom took a flour-sack dish towel out of the drawer and began tearing it into strips. She folded one of the clean, white strips into a square then took a pair of scissors out of the drawer and cut the string that held Flora Mae's hankie to Jo's toe. Blood gushed from the cut. She put one of the squares over the wound and applied pressure with her fingers.

"Is there anything I can do, Mrs. Barkley?" Bobby asked.

"Yes. Ride out to the field and get Mr. Barkley. I may need help."

Bobby swung back onto Flaxen and headed for the field on the run.

"Where's Flora Mae?" Mom asked.

"She's bringing Prince."

"Can she ride him by herself?"

"Sure. She'll be all right. I told her to wait until we were out of sight so Prince wouldn't try to keep up with Flaxen."

In a few minutes, Dad came in from the field.

"I think the bleeding has finally stopped," Mom said.

Dad washed his hands, then came to examine the wound. "This is an ugly, jagged cut. Get me the turpentine, Mama. What were you doing, Jo, trying to cut your toe off?"

"I stepped on a broken brick."

"Where did you find a broken brick?"

"Down in the well on the old von Hoffman place." Jo flinched as Dad applied turpentine to the wound. It stung worse than a hornet.

"What were you doing down in the well? Haven't you been told to stay out of there?"

"Yes, sir, but we thought maybe they hid some treasure down there." Jo was careful not to say it was Bobby's idea. On the way home he had begged her not to tell.

"Give me a clean square, Mama." Dad placed the clean cloth over the wound. "It bled good enough to clean it out so it shouldn't get infected. Now you wrap it up, Mama. You're better at bandaging than I am. And, Jo, the next time you want to go treasure hunting, get permission. This could cost you a trip to the ranch."

Jo spent the rest of the day out on the front porch on her sleeping mat with her foot propped up on three pillows. She kept thinking about what Dad had said about this costing her a trip to the ranch. What did he mean? Was he going to punish her by not letting her go? Or was it that her toe might not be healed? She remembered the time last year she got in a fight with Bobby at school. As if it were yesterday, she could hear Dad say, "Jo, you've got to learn to control that temper of yours. One of these days it's going to get you into real trouble." If Bobby hadn't made her so mad she couldn't think straight, she wouldn't have jumped down in that well today.

When chore time came, Jo got up and hobbled out to the kitchen.

"What are you doing up?" Mom asked.

"It's time to do chores."

"You're not doing chores tonight, nor for the next several days. You've got to keep that toe clean so it won't get infected."

"I'll help Clyde with the chores," Flora Mae volunteered.

For the next few days, Jo was confined to the house. With time to lie around and think, her mind insisted on reliving the accident with Marybel. She felt again the terrible pain and her resentment of Flora Mae. Even helping with the house work brought welcome relief from her tortured thoughts. Each evening Mom changed the bandage and doctored the wound with turpentine. Finally, it was healed enough that Jo could help with the chores.

At breakfast a few days later, Dad asked, "How did Flora Mae get along with the milking this morning?"

"She did great," Jo said, stuffing her mouth full of toast. "She got Old Jersey milked in time to milk Pet."

"Jo, must you always talk with your mouth full?" Mom asked.

"Sorry, Mom, I forgot."

"How's she coming with her riding?"

"Oh, Uncle Frank, I can ride Prince now all by myself, even at a gallop."

"Good." Dad wiped his mouth on his sleeve and pushed back from the table. "It looks like you two are ready for the ranch."

"Yippee." Jo jumped up and danced a jig. She ran to Dad and gave him a hug. "Thanks, Dad. Right after breakfast I'll ride down and tell Bobby."

"When do we have to be ready?" Flora Mae asked.

"You'll leave a week from yesterday," Dad said.

"How are we going to get there, Uncle Frank?"

"Grandpa will take you to your place. Your dad said in his letter he would drive you on over to the ranch."

"How we all gonna fit in Grandpa's Ford coupe?" Jo asked.

"He'll drive our car."

"Well, we'd better start packing," Flora Mae said. "What will we need to take?"

Jo shook her head. It sure wouldn't take her a week to pack.

"Your Aunt Dell will help you figure that out, won't you Mama?"

"Yes, I'll help with that. There'll be time later."

"I'll help with the dishes, Aunt Dell." Flora Mae began clearing the table.

"I'll feed the chickens when I get back from Bobby's." Jo ran out the door.

"Utah's—a pretty, pretty place," a meadowlark greeted her. She whistled back to it.

"What are you so happy about? You have to stay here, but I get to go to Uncle Clint's ranch." She grinned at the meadowlark and ran to the corral to get Prince. Jo thought the sky had never been so blue nor the alfalfa field so pretty, touched with purple blooms. Even the greasewood sparkled. The hurt of losing Marybel seemed to fade as Jo anticipated three weeks on a real ranch, a ranch just like she was going to own someday.

Prince skidded to a stop in Bobby's yard. Shepp, Bobby's dog, barked a greeting, then trotted over to sniff Tippy. Bobby came out of the house, wiping egg from his face with his shirt sleeve.

"Hey, Bobby, we're going to the ranch."

"For sure?"

"Yeah. Dad said so this morning. We leave next Tuesday. That's only about a week."

"Hot ziggity dog! Boy, was I worried. I thought your dad wouldn't let you go after—"

"Yeah. I been sweating it out, too. He's tough on disobedience. Well, I gotta go. I told Mom I'd be right back to feed the chickens." Jo whirled Prince around and thundered out of the yard.

The week dragged by. Flora Mae fussed all week about what she would take. The night before they were going to leave, Jo laid out a few clothes. The next morning, she rolled them in her bed roll. When Grandpa arrived, they already had their bed rolls piled in the back seat of the car. The family gathered around.

"Now be careful," Mom said as she kissed Jo good-bye. "And don't forget your manners."

"Okay, Mom." Jo turned to Clyde. "Take care of Tippy for me."

"Sure, sis."

Tippy came and licked Jo's hand and whined. He seemed to know she was leaving. Jo scratched him behind the ears. "I'll be back," she said. "You be good while I'm gone."

"Have a good time, pardner." Dad tousled Jo's hair. "And try to be some help to your uncle."

"Sure, Dad." Jo grinned and gave him a hug.

Jo and Grandpa got in the front seat. Flora Mae and Bobby climbed in the back with the bed rolls. Grandpa started the motor and they rattled down the driveway. Jo looked back but couldn't see the house for the cloud of dust.

A little before noon Jo said, "Can we stop at the sand dunes for lunch, Grandpa?"

"Sounds good to me," Grandpa said.

They stopped beside the road and spread out the old table cloth Mom had put in their lunch basket. Jo started to bite into a sandwich.

"Wait a minute, Jo. Just because we're having a picnic we don't want to forget to be thankful." Jo put her sandwich down and closed her eyes while Grandpa thanked God for the food and the good trip they were having.

"What kind of flowers are those?" Jo pointed to a patch of white, lily-like flowers waving gracefully in the breeze on slender stems.

"Those are sego lilies," Flora Mae said. "They're the Utah state flower."

"Oh, I remember. We studied about them in school. They were named the state flower because Ute Indians taught the early Mormon settlers to eat the roots."

"Yeah," Bobby said. "The settlers would have starved to death before their crops grew if the friendly Indians hadn't taught them about sego lily roots."

"I see you kids learned your history well. Now we'd better gather up this lunch stuff and get on the road if we want to get to Flora Mae's place before dark."

Just beyond the sand dunes, the car started going bump, bump.

"Oh, no." Grandpa pulled over and stopped.

Seven

"What is it, Grandpa? What happened?" Jo asked.

"I think it's just a flat tire. Let's go have a look." They all piled out of the car.

"Wow, that's flat as a squashed stink bug," Bobby said as they all looked at the right rear tire.

"And smells about as bad," Grandpa added. "You kids find some rocks to block the wheels while I get out the jack and tire iron." Grandpa took the tire off and examined the inner tube. "Here's our problem. Jo, get me the patching kit out of the tool box."

It was dark when they finally arrived at Flora Mae's house. Aunt Bessie had supper waiting for them. After a good night's sleep, Jo was ready to be on the road again, but they had to wait until Uncle Charlie got off work at noon.

After dinner, Flora Mae pulled on the new cowboy boots her folks had bought for her and climbed into the front seat of her dad's Ford roadster. Jo and Bobby squeezed into the rumble seat with the bed rolls. Jo looked at the scuffed up oxfords she'd worn to school all year. Jealousy gnawed at her stomach.

She pushed aside the thought of cowboy boots and set her mind to enjoy the ride up Provo Canyon. The river rippled beside the road and canyon walls towered on either side. Trees and brush grew here and there among the rocks. They drove through Heber Valley with its meadows spread with butter-colored dandelions. About mid-afternoon, they stopped at Strawberry Reservoir and got out to stretch their legs.

"That's the dam your dad helped build, Jo," Uncle Charlie said as they looked out across the reservoir. "Back in 1913 he drove a four horse team on a slip scraper that piled up the dirt to make that dam. On weekends he rode a horse to Heber to court your mom."

"Wow, you mean he rode a horse all that way we've just come from Heber? He must have been some cowboy." Jo tried to imagine riding a horse that far.

"Yep. Every week, all the way in and all the way back for work. Well, we'd better be on our way again or we'll miss out on your Aunt Myrtle's fried chicken."

As they drove past the reservoir, Jo saw bluebells and Indian paintbrush along the road. Just beyond Fruitland, they turned off the main road and headed north.

"Are we almost there, Uncle Charlie?" Jo asked.

"Maybe another hour. We still have to go down Golden Stairs Canyon."

"We're gonna be late for supper," Bobby said. "I'm starved."

"What are we stopping here for?" Jo asked as they slowed almost to a stop.

"We're not stopping. I have to shift into low gear so we won't burn out the brakes on this steep grade. This is Golden Stairs Canyon."

"Look at those rock ledges." Jo pointed to their left at red rocks that looked like giant stair steps up the canyon wall. "That must be how this canyon got its name."

After a steep, winding descent, the road straightened out to cross a bridge.

"This is the Duchesne River," Uncle Charlie said. "And there is Tabiona Valley."

"Oh, how beautiful!" Flora Mae exclaimed.

A mountain valley stretched out before them. The sun hung low over Tabby Mountain as they drove on toward Tabiona. Willows and cottonwoods along the river cast long shadows across meadows of native grass. Higher on the mountain they could see pine trees and juniper with patches of aspen here and there.

Uncle Charlie turned off the main road at Tabiona and drove past the tiny village to turn up Farm Creek Road. They jounced up a winding lane deeply rutted from the spring rains. They couldn't see beyond the next turn because of the brush along the creek. They bounced around one more corner, and there lay the ranch.

The two-story house of weathered boards caught Jo's attention first. An open porch stretched all along the front. It had a hammock at one end with climbing roses nearby. Below the house lay the corrals and a real barn, not like the little straw shed back home. Between the big house and the barn stood a smaller log house with an outhouse behind it. They rumbled across the creek on a wooden bridge and rolled to a stop in the front yard.

Aunt Myrtle came out on the porch drying her hands on her apron. Uncle Clint rushed past her and ran down the steps to open the car door for Flora Mae. He was a little shorter than Dad, with broad shoulders and slightly bowed legs. Jo thought he would look best in a saddle. His shock of red hair reminded her of her own unruly curls. He lifted Jo from the rumble seat and swung her to the ground.

"So these are the cowhands Frank sent me." He gathered both girls in his arms. Turning to Bobby with a handshake, he said, "And this must be Bobby."

"Well, don't stand out there gabbing all day. Bring them in. They must be starved." Aunt Myrtle stood on the porch with her hands on her hips. She was taller than Mom, with black hair and dark, smiling eyes.

Jo climbed the steps, followed by Bobby and Flora Mae. Aunt Myrtle reached out and pulled her into a warm embrace. Jo thought her hands, with their long, slender fingers, looked sturdy enough to spank a wayward child, but gentle enough to mend the broken leg of a tiny bird.

The other three members of the family had come out, but Aunt Myrtle shooed them back into the house.

"We'll have introductions while we eat," she said. "Get washed up and sit. The food's ready and getting cold."

All was quiet while Uncle Clint said a blessing, then everyone began to talk at once. They flooded Jo with questions about the family and the farm down on the flat.

"Whoa up, all you cayuses." Uncle Clint's face crinkled into a grin. "We're forgetting our manners. We haven't even had introductions yet. You were just a little tyke when we last saw you, Jo. Barely walkin'. What's it been, Myrt, ten years?"

"Lands, yes. Rod was only seven, Lorna was three, and Punky wasn't even borned yet."

"Well," Uncle Clint began, "this handsome young man on my right is Rod. He only lacks an inch of catching up with his pa and he's my right hand man here on the ranch." Jo noted the wavy black hair and dark brown eyes. "That dark eyed beauty sitting down there by your Aunt Myrtle is Lorna. She's her mom's main helper, but a fair hand with cattle, too." Lorna's blush turned her rich tan a few shades darker. "And this pipsqueak on the other side of me is Ben, but we call him Punky. He's the only one that didn't get their mother's dark hair and brown eyes. Punk's our wrangler. He'll introduce you to your horses in the morning."

Jo could hardly sit still to eat the rest of her supper. She had a zillion questions she wanted to ask about the ranch, especially about Punky's job of caring for the horses. She didn't have a chance because she had to keep answering questions about the family back home. How was Grandma? Was Grandpa still able to do his own farming? Had Mom regained her strength after that bout with pneumonia last summer? Did Dad think this was going to be a good year for the alfalfa seed? Jo was relieved when Aunt Myrtle got up to start clearing the table. This seemed to be the signal that the family was excused.

"C'mon," Punky said. "I'll show you the horses now. It's too late to ride but we can go look them over."

Jo, Bobby, and Flora Mae followed Punky out to the corrals. They sat on the pole fence, and Punky talked about the horses as if they were personal friends or members of the family.

"That tall red roan is Dad's horse. We call him Strawberry. He comes to Dad's whistle but he plays hard to catch for everyone else. He's the fastest horse on the ranch."

"What about that little buckskin?" Jo asked.

"That's Little Rascal," Punky said. "He was my favorite until I started Chipeta. Little Rascal's high spirited. I think you'll like his quick stops and starts. You'll be riding him."

"Which one's Chipeta?" Bobby asked.

"She's that little black and white pinto. She's a two-year-old filly out of Black Star. I just started her this spring."

"How did she get a name like Chipeta?" Jo asked.

"Bucky and I named her for Chief Ouray's wife."

"Who's Bucky?" Flora Mae wanted to know.

"Oh, he's my Indian friend. You'll meet him. Flora Mae, you'll be riding Chipeta's mother, Black Star. Her specialty is taking care of inexperienced riders. She prefers a slow lope but will go faster if you ask her to."

"A slow lope suits me fine," Flora Mae said.

"Punkeeee. Bed time." Aunt Myrtle's clear voice floated down from the house.

"Coming, Ma," Punky called back. "Bobby, you'll be riding that roan Appie."

"What's an Appie?" Flora Mae asked.

"That's short for Appaloosa," Jo explained. "They're a real tough horse."

"We call him Appie. He's a dependable cow horse, but he'll jump every ditch you come to. Hope you like riding a jump."

"We'll get along," Bobby said.

"The blue roan must be Rod's horse," Jo said as they headed for the house.

"Yeah. That's Roanie. He's the best cutting and roping horse on the ranch."

Back at the house Aunt Myrtle hustled the kids off to bed. "Bobby, you'll sleep in the bunk house with Rod and Punky."

"Is that the little log house between here and the barn?" Bobby asked.

"Yes, we use it when we have an extra hand or two. Jo and Flora Mae, you can have Rod and Punky's room. Now off to bed with you. You'll have a big day tomorrow."

Lorna showed Jo and Flora Mae to a room upstairs.

Jo unrolled her bedroll on one of the cots and crawled between the blankets. She lay awake for a long time trying to fix all the horses' names in her mind and wondering about Bucky. Finally, she drifted off to sleep to dream of Little Rascal.

Eight

When Jo awoke, the morning sun greeted her. She jumped out of bed and pulled on her shirt and overalls. Running her fingers through her tangled curls, she thought about her short red hair and wondered what it would be like to have long black hair like Lorna's. She rummaged through her things to find a comb and stuck it in her pocket. Flora Mae still slept on the cot across the room.

Jo followed the smell of coffee and bacon down the stairs to the kitchen where Aunt Myrtle was turning flapjacks.

"Good morning, Aunt Myrtle."

"Mornin', Jo." Aunt Myrtle turned from the stove to gather Jo in her arms.

"Why didn't you call me?" Jo asked. "I could have helped with chores before breakfast."

"Anybody gets to be a guest for a day or two around here. Then you become one of the hands if you stick around." Aunt Myrtle's chuckle seemed to fill the kitchen with warmth. "You can wash up here in the wash pan with warm water or go out in the yard and wake yourself up with spring water."

"Spring water sounds good to me." Jo took the towel Aunt Myrtle offered and went outside. Water flowed from a pipe into a pool lined with moss-covered rocks, then ran down the hill toward the corrals. Jo splashed the icy water on her face and ran her wet hands through her hair. She took the comb out of her pocket and tugged it through her tangled curls.

The stream beckoned, so she followed it down the hill. It ran across a corner of the corral to form a water hole for the horses before meandering on through the pasture. Jo leaned against the pole fence and called each horse by name, pleased with herself that she could remember them all. Then she went to the barn. Rod and Punky had just finished the milking.

"Good morning, sleepy head," Rod teased. "Why weren't you out here milking cows?"

"Aunt Myrtle says I can be a guest for a day or two." Jo liked Rod. He reminded her of Clyde.

"Well, let's go in and eat those flapjacks," Punky said, "before Ma throws them out."

"Where's Bobby?" Jo asked.

"He was still asleep when we crawled out. I'll go see if I can rouse him." Punky headed for the log bunk house.

"Tell him he's going to miss breakfast. That'll bring him." Jo grinned, thinking how Bobby always seemed to be hungry.

Flora Mae and Lorna were already eating when Rod and Jo got to the house.

"Where's your dad?" Jo asked Flora Mae.

"Aunt Myrtle said he left before sunup."

"Grab a plate and help yourself, Jo," Aunt Myrtle said. "It's every man for himself at breakfast. Your Uncle Clint ate and rode out early this morning."

"Where'd he go?" Rod asked.

"Went over to talk to Buck Too Tall. He wants to know if Buck's missing any cattle this spring."

"Pa told me to try to get a count on our herd while I'm down at the other end fixing fence today."

"You need a lunch?"

"Yeah, I may not be back before supper time."

Punky and Bobby came in. They all ate their fill of flapjacks, bacon, and eggs. Following Rod and Lorna's example, they took their plates and put them on the kitchen counter.

"Shall we help with the dishes?" Flora Mae asked.

"No. You cowpokes go on out and get acquainted with your horses this morning. We'll put you to work in a few days."

At the corral, Punky led out the horses and tied them to the hitch rail. He had the new cowhands curry and brush their own mounts. When he brought a saddle out of the tack room, Jo said, "I'd like to try Little Rascal bareback first, since that's the way I'm used to riding."

"Okay by me. Bring him over to the round pen. Dad said I had to start all of you in there to be sure you're getting along with your horses." Jo led Little Rascal to the round pen. Punky boosted her on, and she rode around a few times at a walk, then at a trot. When she kicked him in the ribs to go faster, Little Rascal went up in the air and came down stiff legged with his head down. Jo shot off over his head and landed sitting in the soft sand. Punky doubled over laughing.

"You hit his buck button," he said.

Jo got up and brushed the sand off her pants. Little Rascal stood there looking at her as if to say, "Wasn't that fun?"

"I'll get you for this, Punky," Jo said. "Now help me back on. I've got to figure this one out."

"It's simple." Punky grinned and boosted Jo back on. "Don't kick him unless you want him to buck. If you want to go fast just lift the reins and squeeze him a little with your legs."

Jo followed Punky's instructions. Little Rascal took off like a hawk diving for a mouse. His stops were just as quick. She rode him in a figure eight and marveled at his smooth turns and his quick response to her leg cues. This was going to be one fun horse to ride.

As they led Little Rascal back to the hitch rail, Punky looked at Jo's worn oxfords.

"Those the only shoes you got?" he asked.

"Yes." Jo kicked a rock and thought of Flora Mae's new cowboy boots.

"Let's go see if Ma can dig up an old pair of boots for you."

They found Aunt Myrtle wiping the kitchen counters and putting away the last of the dishes.

"Ma, do we got an old pair of boots Jo can wear? She'll get hung up in a stirrup with these shoes she's wearing."

"Look in the hall closet. I think there's a pair Lorna outgrew."

Punky rummaged in the closet and came up with a pair of boots that fit Jo.

"What about Bobby?" Jo pulled on Lorna's old boots.

"His high top work shoes'll hold the stirrup okay," Punky said.

Back at the corral, Punky showed the new hands how to saddle their horses. Then they went riding. By noon Jo felt almost as much at home in the saddle as she did riding bareback. After lunch, they lounged around the porch for a while, taking turns in the hammock.

"You ready to ride some more?" Punky asked.

"Sure," Jo and Bobby said at the same time.

"I don't know." Flora Mae rubbed the seat of her pants.

"Would you like to stay here at the ranch with me this afternoon?" Lorna asked. "We'll find something to do."

"Thanks, I'd like that."

Jo, Bobby, and Punky headed for the corral. As they saddled up, Punky said, "I'll take you up Tabby Mountain this afternoon. Chipeta needs the training. So far I've only ridden her around the ranch."

"Oh, boy. I been wanting to see what it's like up on the mountain." Jo tightened Little Rascal's cinch and swung into the saddle.

They rode down the Farm Creek road and past Tabiona. At the bridge across the Duchesne River, Chipeta balked. Jo watched to see what Punky would do. He didn't whip her or kick her. He let her turn and go away from the bridge. Each time he brought her back, he talked to her and patted her on the neck. Finally, she put one foot on the bridge before turning away. The next time they approached, she skittered across.

"Where did you learn to train horses?" Jo asked as they rode up Tabby Mountain.

"From Buck Too Tall."

"Who's Buck Too Tall?"

"Bucky's grandpa. He's tribal chairman and the best rancher on the reservation."

"That's a funny name," Bobby said.

"The way I heard it his father was the tallest brave in his band so they started calling him Too Tall. It got passed down as the family name."

A light breeze ruffled Jo's hair as they rode in silence up the winding dirt road that climbed steadily up the mountain. The afternoon sun was warm on her face as she soaked up the beauty of the trees and wild flowers. Bird songs filled the air.

"I'll have to get acquainted with some of those birds," she said. "Do you know any of their names, Punky?"

"Naw, I never pay much attention to birds. Too busy with horses. Ma knows them all; the wild flowers, too."

Time passed quickly for Jo with a whole new world to explore. She thrilled to the fragrance and color of red and blue and yellow wild flowers. So different from the greasewood and skunk weed back home. Her ears strained to catch every new bird song, but she missed the lilting whistle of the meadowlark.

The breeze picked up as they topped out on a ridge and stopped to let their horses blow.

"This here's Windy Ridge," Punky said. "Probably far enough for today. Besides, my belly says it's getting close to supper time. We better head back. Ma don't like it if we're late for supper."

As they rode down the mountain, Jo noted trails going off the main road into the forest. She'd explore them another day.

At supper that night, all the talk was about the dance the next evening. Jo found out Uncle Clint's family band played for the Friday night dances in the school house. Uncle Clint played the drums and Aunt Myrtle the fiddle or piano. Rod played guitar mostly, but also sang and played trumpet and harmonica. Lorna played piano and sang.

"You ain't heard nothin' till you've heard Rod and Lorna sing a duet," Punky said.

"What do you play, Punky?" Jo asked.

"I just play with Bucky and try to keep Lorna out of trouble with those handsome cowboys." Punky grinned at his sister. Lorna threw a biscuit at him.

"Will Buck Too Tall be there?" Jo asked.

"Yes, everybody goes to the Friday night dances," Aunt Myrtle said.

"Except the drunks," Uncle Clint added. "The Bishop makes sure they're not welcome. It's a time of good clean family fun. You'll enjoy it."

Jo went to sleep that night excited about meeting an Indian for the first time. She hoped she could be friends with Buck Too Tall.

Nine

"Punky, you take your crew down to the lower pasture this morning and bring up that bunch. We'll see if these cowpokes know how to stay with a horse while it's working cattle. It's a little different from herding milk cows." Uncle Clint smiled at Jo as he pushed back from the breakfast table. "Then you kids can have the rest of the day off. Just remember to start the evening chores early so you'll all have time to get ready for the dance."

As the others went out the door, Jo lingered behind to talk to Aunt Myrtle.

"What'll I wear, Aunt Myrtle? I didn't bring a dress because Mom said you didn't have a church to go to here." Jo remembered how Flora Mae had made such a fuss about packing. Now she wished she had given it a little more thought.

"Put on a clean shirt and overalls and polish up those old boots of Lorna's. You'll be fine." Aunt Myrtle's smile was like sunshine in a protected nook on a cold spring day. She had a way of making everything seem all right.

Jo raced down the hill to the corral. Punky and the others had the horses saddled. They rode through the upper pasture. Jo noticed a hay field of native grass just across the fence to their left, so different from the alfalfa fields back home. When they came to a ditch, Appie gathered himself and leaped across. Bobby rode the jump smoothly.

"Hey, Bobby, if you keep practicing, you're going to make a horseman yet," she teased.

"At least I haven't got dumped." Jo took his dig with a grin.

At the lower pasture, they bunched the cattle and started them toward the corrals. One cow darted out of the herd and headed for the willows. When Little Rascal whirled to head her off, Jo rode the whirl with ease. But when he started dodging back and forth jump for jump with the cow, she felt like his front end faded out from under her. She gave him a loose rein and grabbed the saddle horn. Little Rascal could take care of the cow. Her job was to stay in the saddle. Now she knew what Uncle Clint meant. This *was* different from herding milk cows.

That evening as the girls dressed for the dance, Flora Mae put on her yellow gingham dress with the fitted bodice and full skirt and carefully arranged her black, Shirley Temple curls. For a fleeting moment, Jo wished she were as pretty as Flora Mae. She shrugged and pulled on her clean shirt and overalls and Lorna's polished, old boots.

At the school house, Uncle Clint set up his drums on the platform at one end of the gym. He and his band were warming up when in walked a tall, swarthy Indian with sharply chiseled features. He had the broad shoulders and slender hips of a cowboy and wore jeans and a western shirt with a beaded buckskin vest. A hint of gray streaked his black, neatly trimmed hair. Uncle Clint laid down his drum sticks and came to shake hands.

"Jo, this is my friend Buck Too Tall. He's a horse trainer. I think you two will find a lot to talk about."

"You don't look like an Indian," Jo blurted. She felt her face get hot. "I...I mean, the only Indians I've seen were in the movies."

Buck Too Tall's laugh was like the ripple of a mountain stream. "Guess I don't look much like the movie Indians."

"Well, I'd better get back and start up the band. I'm leaving you in good hands, Jo." Uncle Clint smiled at her and strolled back to the stage.

Buck Too Tall escorted Jo to one of the bleachers.

A crowd gathered, women and girls in their bright cotton dresses, men and boys in jeans and western shirts with bandanas around their necks. The strains of a lively foxtrot rose above the clumping of boots and chatter of friends greeting one another. Soon couples were twirling around the floor in a sea of rhythm and color.

"Do you dance?" Buck asked.

"No. I don't know how. Mom frowns on dancing. I'd rather hear how you train horses."

"Your uncle tells me you are quite a little horse woman. Something about being named grand champion at the county fair."

"That was mostly because of Prince, the pony Grandpa gave me. Grandpa had him already well trained. Punky says you're teaching him to train horses."

"He learns by watching. He's been hanging around with my grandson, Bucky, since they were four. That's Bucky over there with Punky now."

Jo glanced in the direction Buck indicated. There at the end of the bleachers near the coat rack, two heads, one black and one straw colored, bent over some treasure known only to young boys. Nearby, a tall girl with black, curly hair faced a short, confused looking boy. Jo chuckled. Flora Mae was trying to teach Bobby to dance!

Jo turned back to her new friend. "How did you learn to train horses, Mr. Too Tall?"

"You may call me Buck. Everybody does. I guess I grew up knowing horses. In the old days, Indians put a papoose on a colt as soon as the colt was strong enough to hold him. As the colt got stronger, a bigger papoose rode him. That way, when the horse was strong enough to hold a brave, he was no longer afraid of men."

"So the papooses were the real horse trainers?"

"Well, you might say that. You see, the main reason a horse gives trouble is because he's afraid. So you need to win his trust."

"Why do some horses buck so much the first time they are ridden?"

"It's because the rider hasn't taken time to build that trust."

"I guess the cowboys of the old west just didn't take time with a new horse. Maybe they thought it was more fun to ride a bronco."

"Maybe, but I think they didn't have that much time to spend with each horse. You see, they rounded up the horses off the range and had to have a whole string of saddle broncs ready to ride right away."

Buck told how horses could be trained to respond to leg signals and shifting of the rider's weight. Jo could have listened all evening.

"They're starting a slow waltz," Buck said. "If you'll excuse me, I'd better go dance with my wife."

"Thanks for taking time to talk to me, Buck. I've really enjoyed it. I hope I can learn to train horses. Someday I'm going to own a ranch."

"Good luck, Jo. You'll make a good horse trainer."

Rod and Lorna stepped to the front of the platform and began singing "Moonlight on the Colorado." Punky was right. They sure could sing. Jo spent the rest of the evening watching the dancers and thinking about her talk with Buck.

The next morning Punky said he was going to spend the day with Bucky. Jo, Bobby, and Flora Mae would be on their own. That suited Jo fine. She talked over plans with Bobby and Flora Mae.

"Aunt Myrtle, may we pack a lunch today? Bobby and Flora Mae and I want to go up Tabby Mountain and see how many birds we can identify."

"That's fine with me. With all of you out from under foot, Lorna and I can get the house cleaned up for Sunday. Just be back in time for supper."

They saddled up and followed the road until they came to a trail beside a creek. Jo led the way along the stream as it meandered through a pine forest. Soon they came to an aspen grove. A thicket of wild roses bloomed along the creek. Jo saw a splash of bright blue flit from the rose bushes to an aspen tree.

"Let's stop here," she said. "This will be a good place to rest and watch for birds."

They watered their horses and tied them to trees. Then they found comfortable seats on a little outcropping of moss-covered rocks. Jo looked through her book to find a small, blue bird. She looked up to see a bird fly from the tree to hover low over the ground. Suddenly, it dropped down and flew back up with a bug in its beak.

"It's a mountain bluebird," she whispered. "See, here's its picture. It must have a nest in that hole in the tree. It's feeding its young."

"Wish we could get up there to see the little birds," Bobby said.

"So do I, but there's no way."

"There are a lot of small birds in the rose bushes," Flora Mae said.

"Yeah, but they look so much alike I can't find them in my book."

"I'm hungry. Let's eat." Without waiting for an answer, Bobby got up to get their sandwiches from the saddle bag. After lunch they rode on up the trail.

"Do you think we should ride this far from the ranch? What if we see a mountain lion?"

"Oh, Flora Mae, stop worrying," Jo said. "Mountain lions only hunt at night. I want to see what's on top of the mountain."

The trail became steep and rocky. Jo could see a rock outcropping above the brush.

"Let's tie our horses here and go have a look."

As they scrambled up over the rocks, they could see a faint trail that seemed to disappear into a rose bramble. Jo led the way through the thorny bushes. They came out into a small clearing at the mouth of a cave.

"Let's go see what's inside," Bobby said.

"I don't think we should." Flora Mae's voice trembled. "What if there are mountain lions in there?"

Jo had already gone through the small opening into a large room.

"C'mon." Bobby grabbed Flora Mae's hand and followed Jo into the cave.

In the dim light they could barely make out a few arrow heads and some eagle feathers on the floor. Jo stubbed her toe on something hard. As she stooped to see what it was, a shadow concealed it. She looked up. A big Indian blocked their exit. He wore a brightly colored blanket and his black hair hung in two long braids in front of his shoulders.

Jo tried to melt into the wall. Her knees shook and her heart beat seemed to shatter the silence of the cave. Despite the coolness of the air, sweat trickled down her face.

"Forbidden cave," the Indian said.

"We didn't know." Jo tried to keep her voice steady.

"Chief Tabby's grave. Chief be much angry."

"Just let us go. We won't come again. I promise." Jo felt like her voice came from somewhere back in the cave.

"If you go, white man come. Sacred Cave of Ute people not be secret anymore."

"We won't tell anyone. Honest." Jo's mind raced faster than Uncle Clint's horse, Strawberry. "Here. I'll give you a lock of my hair. If the white men come, you can find me and take me to your chief." Jo took out her pocket knife and cut off one of her red curls.

This seemed to satisfy the Indian. He took the lock of hair and let them go. They raced to their horses and rode down the mountain like rabbits chased by a coyote. At the river, a safe distance from the cave, Jo reined in and slid off her horse.

"Don't stop here." Flora Mae was quaking like an aspen. "That Indian's apt to follow us. I won't feel safe until we're back at the ranch."

"Yeah, shouldn't we get back?" Bobby asked.

"I've got to get myself together." Jo collapsed on the river bank. She scooped up the cold water, splashed it on her face, and ran her fingers through her tousled curls. "Does it show where I cut my hair?"

"Not much," Flora Mae said.

"Where'd you get that crazy idea of giving him a lock of your hair?" Bobby asked.

"I don't know. It just popped into my head, but it worked."

"Well, that's as close to getting scalped as I'd ever want." Bobby shuddered as he settled himself on the river bank by Jo.

"We'd better keep mum about that cave," Jo said, "or we'll really get scalped."

"Indians don't scalp people anymore," Flora Mae scoffed.

"I know that, but still we'd better keep quiet or we'll be in more trouble than a mouse in an owl's burrow. If we squeal and that Indian finds out, he'll be after us for sure."

They all agreed and sealed it with a six-hand shake.

Ten

"Bucky and me ate a potguts squirrel today," Punky said as he shoved in a mouthful of potatoes and gravy.

"Ma, does he have to tell us these things at the supper table?" Lorna made a face at Punky.

"When else would he tell us? This is the only time we're all together anymore." Aunt Myrtle brushed a lock of hair from her face and smiled at Punky.

"What's a potguts squirrel?" Jo asked.

"It's a ground squirrel. About like the quimps you have down your way," Uncle Clint said.

"How'd you catch him?" Bobby asked. "Did you drown him out like Jo and I do the quimps?"

"We set a snare over his hole. Bucky's grandpa taught him how."

"Did you eat him raw?" Flora Mae looked like she was about to gag.

"Naw, we built a fire and cooked him till he popped. That's how you tell when they're done."

"Yuck." Flora Mae's fork clattered to her plate and she covered her mouth with her hand.

"What did he taste like?" Jo hoped Punky would keep talking so no one would ask about their day.

"Like rabbit, only greasier."

Uncle Clint's eyes twinkled as he listened to the conversation.

"May I be excused to start the dishes?" Lorna looked at her mother who smiled and nodded.

"I'll come help you," Flora Mae said.

"What are you and Bucky going to do in the morning?" Bobby looked up from cutting his steak.

"We're gonna track a bobcat."

"Not tomorrow, Punky," his dad said.

"Oh, I forgot. Tomorrow's Sunday."

"What do you do on Sunday?" Bobby asked.

"After morning chores, we gather around the piano in the front room and sing hymns. Then we study the Bible together," Punky said. "It's fun because Dad knows how to make the Bible stories interesting."

"Oh, you have your own Sunday School? Does anyone else come?" Jo wondered if Buck Too Tall and his family would be there.

"No. Most everyone else in the valley is Mormon. They have their own meetings," Punky said.

"Why don't you go to their church? Don't you like them?" Bobby asked.

"Of course we like them," Aunt Myrtle said. "Many of them are our good friends. It's just that we don't believe like they do."

"Yes," Uncle Clint added, "we agreed when we took this job that we'd have Sunday School here at home so our kids would get the teaching we believe to be the truth."

"What do you mean, Uncle Clint, when you took this job? Isn't this your ranch?"

"Oh, no, Jo. We just run the ranch for a Mormon bishop who lives in Heber. When we first came, he and his family lived in this house, and we lived in the log house. I came as a ranch hand, and your Aunt Myrtle was cook. When his wife became ill, they moved to Heber and he asked me to run the ranch for him."

When chores were finished the next morning, they all gathered in the living room. Jo liked Sunday School at the ranch. Aunt Myrtle played lively hymns and everyone sang. Uncle Clint made the Bible lesson interesting just like Punky said. After the lesson, Aunt Myrtle and Lorna put Sunday dinner on the table. Jo and Flora Mae helped.

"Okay, men," Uncle Clint said after dinner, "Sunday afternoon is cook's day off. We get the privilege of doing the dishes." Rod, Punky, and Bobby all pitched in and helped Uncle Clint.

Aunt Myrtle picked up a book and went to the hammock on the porch. Jo followed her.

"Aunt Myrtle, do you think it would be all right if I rode over and visited the Too Talls this afternoon?"

"Sure, Jo, I don't know why not. Punky and Bobby have something cooked up and Lorna has invited Flora Mae to spend the afternoon with her. You'd be welcome to join them, but if you'd rather go to the Too Talls, that would be fine."

Jo went to the corral and caught Little Rascal. As she brushed and saddled him, she struggled with her problem. How could she find out about the sacred cave without letting Buck know she'd been there?

Jo found Buck out by the corral. He was just turning in a horse he had been working.

"Well, what gives me the honor of a visit from my best friend's niece?" He took Little Rascal's reins as Jo swung down from the saddle.

"Aunt Myrtle said I could come over and visit you. I want to learn more about your people."

"Let's go up to the house and sit a spell. I enjoy spinning yarns about my people." Buck tied Little Rascal to the hitch rail and loosened his cinch.

The house was a substantial wood frame building much like Uncle Clint's house. Jo noticed a strange smell as they climbed the steps to the porch. She wondered what it was but didn't think it polite to ask.

"Excuse me," Buck said. "I'll be right back."

Jo looked out over a meadow dotted with wild flowers. There were patches of red Indian paint brush, blue lupine, and a yellow flower she didn't recognize. She took out her pocket knife and began to sharpen it.

When Buck returned, he set two tall glasses of lemonade on a stand beside Jo's chair. Then he handed her a pair of buckskin gloves.

"I thought you'd like to see some of my wife's work," he said. "She tanned the deer hide and smoked it. That's what gives it the rich buckskin color."

Jo took the soft gloves in her hand and lifted them to her nose. She'd never smelled anything like this before. She couldn't describe the smell, but she liked it.

"Oh these are beautiful," she exclaimed. "But I thought all tanned buckskin was this color."

"No," Buck explained. "The unsmoked hides come out white."

Jo laid the gloves on the stand and picked up her glass of lemonade.

"I see you like a sharp knife, Jo. Aren't you afraid you'll cut yourself?" Buck pulled up a chair and sat down.

"My dad says to always treat a gun as if it were loaded and always treat a knife as if it were sharp. So I figure I may as well keep mine sharp. A dull knife isn't much good."

"Well, you're right about that. A rancher always needs to keep a sharp knife handy."

"You sure have a beautiful view here," Jo said.

"We like it." They enjoyed a comfortable silence. Then Buck asked, "What have you heard about my people?"

"In school we read about Chief Walker and the Walker War. It sounded like he was a really bad Indian."

"Wakara—" Sorrow clouded Buck's face and a faraway look came into his eyes. Jo wondered if she had said the wrong thing. She waited for Buck to speak.

"My people were a proud and angry people in the days of Wakara. He was our hero back then." Buck looked at Jo with sadness in his eyes.

"You probably know the Mormons came and settled in the Wasatch Valley in the 1840s."

"Yes, we studied about that."

"Their leader, Brigham Young, tried to make friends with my people. Some of them accepted the Mormon religion and became farmers. Many of the Utes didn't want to change. They liked moving here and there and living off the land. When white men killed their deer, the Weenoochew, the Old People, thought it was only fair to kill their cattle. Then some white men killed two Ute warriors, so Wakara led raiding parties against white villages."

"I never heard it explained this way."

"It was not good, all the killing that went on. Many of my people died, too."

They sat in silence for a while. Jo tried to understand how Buck's people must have felt when white men came and took over their hunting grounds.

Finally she asked, "Did you know Chief Tabby?"

"Yes. Tabby was one of Wakara's brothers. He didn't share his older brother's warlike spirit. Tabby became a friend of Brigham Young and counseled his people to try to get along with their white brothers.

"I was about your age when Bishop Murdock invited Chief Tabby and some of the other chiefs to Heber. We were already living on the reservation, but some of our braves were still making raids on the settlements in Heber Valley. The women of Heber put on a big feast for us. Then the men sat around and smoked the peace pipe. Chief Tabby signed a treaty that put an end to the raids in that valley."

"How old were you when Chief Tabby died?" Jo closed her knife and put it back in her pocket.

"I don't know exactly how old I am," Buck said. "My people didn't keep records back then, but I suppose I was in my forties. He died over by White Rocks, and many of my people went from here to his burial."

"Where is White Rocks?"

"It's over on the eastern side of the reservation. Close to fifty miles from here. It is said Chief Tabby was 104 years old when he died. He'd been blind for a number of years. I remember that day well. They brought many of his personal belongings to the grave and buried them there with him. Some of the braves rounded up forty of his horses and led or drove them to the scene. The horses were shot over the grave."

Jo felt a stab of pain as she thought of Marybel. "What a waste of horses," she said.

"Yes," Buck agreed, "but that was the way of the Weenoochew, the Old People."

Jo had a lot to think about as she rode back to the ranch. Buck said Chief Tabby was buried near White Rocks. Why had the Indian said he was buried in the sacred cave?

Eleven

"Let's play 'No Bears Out Tonight,'" Punky suggested, when the chores were done that evening. "I'll get Rod and Lorna to play with us."

"How do you play?" Flora Mae asked.

"One person is the bear," Jo explained. "The rest stay home and hide their eyes while the bear goes and hides. Then we all venture out away from home singing, 'No bears out tonight.' The bear jumps out from his hiding place and tries to catch us as we all run for home."

"The porch would make a good home," Bobby said.

"But it's almost dark," Flora Mae objected. "How will we see the bear? It will be scary."

"That's what makes it fun." Jo skipped a small pebble across the yard. "This is the only time of day to play 'No Bears Out Tonight.'"

"Rod will be the bear first," Punky said as he came from the house with Rod and Lorna.

"Okay, all you little children, get up on the porch and hide your eyes and count to one hundred."

"By fives or by tens?" Jo asked.

"By ones, and slowly." Rod ran off to hide.

They all counted out loud to one hundred. Then Lorna called out, "Ready or not, here we come." They scattered out over the yard singing, "No bears out tonight." Flora Mae stayed near home. Rod jumped from behind the rose bush at the corner of the house. Flora Mae screamed and scrambled back up on the porch. Then Rod took out after Jo. She led him on a merry chase down around the barn and back up toward the house. At the bunk house, Rod caught her, but everyone else got in free.

While the others counted, Jo hid behind the outhouse. The game continued with much screaming and laughing until Aunt Myrtle came out on the porch and called, "All you bears and children, it's time to hit the hay. There's work to be done tomorrow."

The next morning Uncle Clint gave his instructions for the day. "Rod, we'll bring in the cows and calves from the spring range first. That way they'll have a few days to rest before we start the drive. Punky, you ride over and see if any of our cattle have strayed into Too Talls' herd. Jo, you, Bobby, and Flora Mae will help Rod. You kids be sure to stay on your horses. Those range cows can be pretty protective of their little ones this time of year."

It was slow work driving the cows and calves out of the brush and willows along the creek. Jo would drive one cow out only to have her head back into the willows bellowing for a calf she had hidden there. Flora Mae worked with the ones they had driven out, trying to keep them bunched. Sometimes a cow would plunge across the creek. Bobby had to dodge willows as Appie jumped the creek after her.

Rod finally gave the word to start the cattle toward the ranch. They were beginning to move when a cow darted out of the herd. Black Star whirled to head her off, and Flora Mae lost her balance and went flying. She screamed as the cow ran with head down right for her. Jo leaned forward, lifted the reins, and aimed Little Rascal at the cow. They turned her just before she reached Flora Mae.

"Whew, that was close. Good job," Jo said as she patted Little Rascal's neck.

"Are you hurt?" Bobby asked.

"I don't know." Flora Mae staggered to her feet and seemed to be in a daze.

"You'd better go back to the ranch and let Ma look you over," Rod said. "Can you get back on your horse?"

"I think so."

"Bobby, you go with her and see that she gets to the house all right. Jo and I will bring in the cattle." Rod helped Flora Mae back on Black Star and handed the reins to Bobby. Flora Mae grasped the saddle horn with both hands as Bobby led her horse back to the ranch house.

The cattle had begun to scatter. It took some hard riding for Jo and Rod to get them rounded up again and headed for the ranch.

"That was quick thinking and fancy riding, Jo," Rod said as they trailed behind the cows.

"I'm just glad Little Rascal is so responsive," Jo said. "He's fast, too. I'd like to see him race Bobby's horse, Flaxen."

"Bobby has a fast horse?"

"Yeah, he always wins the races back home. I'm kinda worried about Flora Mae."

"You think she was injured?"

"No. I think she's going to be afraid to ride anymore. She had a bad experience with my old horse, Marybel."

"What happened?"

"I'd rather not talk about it." Jo brushed a tear from her eye. Even now she couldn't think about Marybel without the old hurt returning. Somehow her feelings toward Flora Mae were still entangled in that hurt.

At supper that evening, the talk turned to missing cattle.

"Punky, did you find any of our cattle in Buck's herd?" his dad asked.

"No, but Buck said he's missing some."

"Buck wouldn't steal your cattle, would he, Uncle Clint?"

"No, Jo. Our fence was busted down this spring. We thought before we got it fixed some of our herd might have strayed over there. Our property line borders the reservation."

"What did you find out at the other ranches, Dad?" Rod asked.

"They all seem to be missing a few head. The worst of it is they're beginning to talk about thievin' Indians. This could get ugly."

"If Indians were doing it, they wouldn't steal from Buck, would they?"

"Well, Jo, they might. You see, some of the Indians are jealous of Buck and others who have become successful ranchers. They act like anyone who has adopted white men's ways is a traitor."

"Why don't the other Indians have good ranches like Buck?"

"They'd rather go hunting and fishing."

The rest of the week they gathered cattle. Flora Mae rode in the mornings. Jo noticed she didn't even try to head off a cow or calf that was straying. Just rode along behind the herd. At least she was still willing to ride. By noon she looked tuckered out and Aunt Myrtle said she should rest.

Jo had time to think while they drove the cattle to the ranch. She wondered about Buck Too Tall. Surely, he told her the truth about Chief Tabby's burial place. Then what about the secret cave?

Each evening Uncle Clint said the tension was getting worse among the ranchers. Some were saying they should call in the Feds.

"We can't call in the Feds and accuse the Indians of stealing our cattle when we don't have any evidence," he said.

"We can't accuse anyone until we have evidence," Rod said.

Jo thought again of the secret cave and the Indian who had told them to stay away. She had to have a private council with Bobby and Flora Mae.

"Aunt Myrtle, may we go for a walk up Farm Creek?" Jo asked after supper.

"Sure. I'll go with you. The dishes can wait."

"Oh, that would be great." Jo hoped she wasn't telling a lie. She wanted to learn about the wild flowers and birds. But right now what she wanted even more was to talk to Bobby and Flora Mae alone.

Aunt Myrtle knew all the wild flowers. She could also name most of the birds. The walk was fun, but Jo had to go to bed wrestling with her thoughts. Should they go back up and try to find out what was going on at the cave? Surely it wasn't Chief Tabby's grave as the Indian had said. Should she tell Uncle Clint about it? What about her promise not to go back? She finally drifted off to sleep trying to place a vaguely familiar smell she had noticed while in the cave.

Jo was restless all day Sunday. She made several attempts to get Bobby and Flora to herself, but it never worked. That evening Punky invited everybody to the round pen.

"I have a show for you." He grinned.

"What kind of a show?" Jo asked.

"Come on, you'll see."

Punky put a halter on Little Rascal and led him into the round pen. After closing the gate, he took off the halter and hung it on the fence. Then he grabbed Little Rascal's mane and swung on.

"Watch out, he'll buck with you," Jo said.

"Only if I kick him." Punky grinned at Jo and started Little Rascal on a walk around the round pen. Soon he had him galloping in figure eights, doing sliding stops, and quick turns.

"How does he do that without a bridle or even a rope?" Flora Mae asked.

"He does it with leg signals and shifting his body weight," Jo said. "Buck Too Tall told me about it."

Everybody clapped and cheered as Punky galloped Little Rascal up to the gate and brought him to a sliding stop.

Twelve

Monday morning Uncle Clint sent Rod and Punky out to scour the brush to see if they could find any more strays.

"You three are on your own. Just try to stay out of trouble." He smiled at Jo as he put on his hat and left.

"We're going for a ride, Aunt Myrtle," Jo said as the three friends walked out the door.

"Okay. Come back when you get hungry."

While they brushed and saddled their horses, Jo told Bobby and Flora Mae about her visit with Buck.

"We're gonna have to ride back up to the secret cave," Jo said.

"We can't do that," Flora Mae objected. "We promised the Indian we wouldn't come back."

"Yeah," Bobby added, "what if we get caught again?"

"We won't go to the cave. We'll hide in the rocks up above where we can see what's going on."

"Shouldn't we tell Uncle Clint?" Flora Mae asked.

"We can't tell anybody yet. Buck told me they buried Chief Tabby over by White Rocks."

"Then what do you think's going on?" Bobby climbed aboard Appie.

"I don't know." Jo checked Black Star's cinch and held her while Flora Mae mounted. "I've been trying to place a smell I noticed while we were at the cave," she said as she swung onto Little Rascal. "This morning I figured it out. The ashes of a dead campfire."

"Who would build a campfire at a grave?" Flora Mae shuddered.

"That's just it. I don't think it is Chief Tabby's grave." Jo led the way out onto Farm Creek Road. "Another thing, when we were in the cave, I stubbed my toe on something hard. Maybe it's a running iron."

"What's a running iron?" Flora Mae asked.

"It's a iron rustlers use to change brands on cattle they steal."

They put their horses on a lope, then slowed them to a walk as they rode past Tabiona.

Bobby shifted in his saddle to face Jo. "You think the Indians are stealing the cattle?"

"I don't know, but we've got to ride back up there and see what we can find out."

"Maybe Buck Too Tall's involved," Flora Mae suggested as the three of them rode up Tabby Mountain.

"But he's missing cattle, too," Bobby pointed out.

"That could just be a cover up."

"I don't think so," Jo said. "If he were in on it, he'd know about the Indian who said the secret cave was Chief Tabby's grave. He wouldn't have told me they buried Chief Tabby over by White Rocks."

"Well, if your suspicions are right, Jo, it sure looks like thieving Indians." It irritated Jo that Flora Mae seemed happy to place the blame on the Indians.

Before they got close to the cave, Jo left the dirt road and led the way up a mountain stream. A dense growth of willows screened them from the trail.

"Someone's comin'," Jo said.

"I don't hear anything." Bobby cupped his right hand around his ear.

"I don't either, but look at Little Rascal's ears." Her horse had lifted his head and pointed both ears forward. Jo swung from the saddle and stepped to Little Rascal's head. She stroked his nose and whispered to him. "Easy there, boy. You be quiet. We don't want anyone to know we're here. You two try to keep your horses quiet," she cautioned.

"We better go back to the ranch." Flora Mae's voice trembled like the aspen leaves along the creek.

"We can't go now, just when we're gonna find out about that secret cave." They waited quietly as the sound of a horse's hooves on the trail grew louder then faded away.

"He's headed for the cave, all right," Jo said. "Let's ride around on the back side and find a good place to hide our horses."

Jo and Little Rascal picked their way carefully through the juniper and pinion pine up a steep slope. Jo judged they were about even with the mouth of the cave when they came to a faint trail that led into a secluded valley. They rode down the trail into a grove of aspen trees.

"We'll tie our horses here," Jo said. "Then we'll climb up the hill. That should put us in the rocks above the cave."

"What if there are rattle snakes up in those rocks?" Flora Mae had turned white. Jo remembered how she'd frozen up on them on the hay stack.

"We'll have to keep our eyes open. Just be careful where you put your hands. Our boots and pants will protect our legs." Jo led the way up the steep hill side. Lorna's old cowboy boots worked well in the saddle, but they weren't good for climbing over rocks. More than once Jo wanted to stop and take them off, but she needed the protection.

Before they reached the top, they could hear voices. Jo turned and put her finger over her lips. They stopped to listen but couldn't make out what the men were saying. Carefully the adventurers worked their way on up and peeked over a big boulder. Three rough-looking white men apparently had just arrived. They were still on their horses. The Indian, dressed in jeans, western shirt, and cowboy hat, came out of the cave to meet them.

"Why did you turn those kids loose?" one of the white men demanded. "They could tell someone and mess up our whole operation."

"Don't worry, Boss. They won't be any problem. I scared them good," the Indian bragged.

Jo pulled on her ear. Hm, no blanket, no braids, even his talk was fake. He speaks good English.

"If they go blabbing to Clint Barkley, or even Buck Too Tall, our goose is cooked."

"They won't. That little red headed niece of Clint Barkley's gave me a lock of her hair in pledge that she wouldn't tell anyone." The Indian laughed. "I had them thinking this was Chief Tabby's grave for real."

"If they come snooping around here causing trouble, I'll skin you alive and hang you out to dry." He swung from his horse and handed the reins to one of the other men. They both dismounted and led the horses off the trail into the trees. Just as Boss and the Indian started into the cave, Flora Mae sneezed.

"What was that?" Boss demanded.

"We better make a run for our horses." Jo sped down the rocky hill without waiting for an answer. Bobby followed at her heels. A scream from Flora Mae brought them to a halt.

"Now what?" Jo turned to see Flora Mae perched on a rock, her face as white as the alkali back home.

"A rattlesnake."

"Stay still. Don't move." Jo picked up a rock and scrambled back up the hill. "Where is it?"

"Right there." Flora Mae pointed to a big snake stretched out full length at the base of the rock.

"Oh, for cryin' out loud," Jo exploded, "that's only a blow snake. And he isn't even coiled. Come on, Flora Mae, the rustlers are going to catch us."

"That's right, Missy Red Hair." Jo looked up just as the Indian grabbed her arm.

"Let me go," Jo yelled and pounded the Indian with her free hand. "When Uncle Clint finds out about this, you'll be in big trouble."

"Oh, a little spitfire. She's got a temper to go with that red hair." The Indian laughed as he kept a rough grip on Jo's arm. The other men grabbed Bobby and Flora Mae.

"We'll take them to the cave," Boss said. "We can tie them up and decide later whether to shoot them for the vultures or leave them to the mountain lions."

The men dumped them in the back of the cave and tied their hands and feet. Jo heard them leave. Her stomach knotted in fear. The men must be leaving them here for the mountain lions.

After a while she heard them come back and start a fire. Soon the smell of boiling meat floated into the cave.

"I'm starved," Bobby whispered.

"They won't bother to feed us," Flora Mae said.

"Shh. They're starting to talk. You two forget about your stomachs and listen. Maybe we can find out what's going on."

"What good will it do?" Flora Mae asked. "We'll never get out of here alive."

The three friends couldn't see the men, but they could hear them arguing.

"I say shoot them now and get it over with," one man said.

"Don't be a fool! If we get caught, we'll hang for murder. I say leave them here in the cave for the mountain lions to find."

"When Clint Barkley finds out his niece is missing, he'll turn this mountain upside down to find her."

"Old Too Tall has taken quite a shine to her, too," the Indian said.

"Dratted kids. Why'd they have to come up here poking around anyway?"

"Well, Injun, you'd better take them some of that rabbit stew. We may as well fatten them up for the mountain lions."

Flora Mae started to whimper. "Shush," Jo whispered between clenched teeth. "Don't give them the satisfaction of knowing we're scared. We'll listen and find out all we can. I've got an idea how we can get loose. Our only chance is to make them think we're helpless so they'll go off and leave us here alone. Be quiet now. The Indian's coming with food."

"Here, Missy Red Hair," the Indian said. "Here's food for you and your friends. Mountain lions like fat children."

"Please," Jo begged. "Don't you have any sympathy for helpless children?"

"I used up all my sympathy for you when I let you go the first time." The Indian threw an old blanket over them. "The boss says for you to sleep now."

"We better pretend we're asleep," Flora Mae whispered after the Indian went back to join the other men.

"Yeah," Jo agreed, "but keep your ears open."

All was quiet for a long time. It was dark and spooky. Jo could hear a drip, drip, drip coming from somewhere deeper in the cave. It was hard to keep alert. Finally, the men began to talk.

"Go see if those pesky kids are asleep, Injun," Boss said. "We don't want them hearing our plans."

"It won't make no difference. They're not going anywhere." When the Indian came to check on them, Jo, Bobby, and Flora Mae lay very still and breathed as if they were sleeping.

"They're out for the night," the Indian reported.

"Okay, you guys got this straight? We wait here till it gets good and dark. Then we ride out and get the cattle started. We'll drive them down through Chuck Hollow. By the time the moon comes up, we'll be down along Red Creek where there's good cover. Then we can follow the creek down to Red Creek Reservoir. The truck's going to meet us there just before daylight."

"What about the kids?" one of the men asked.

"We'll leave them where they are. By the time Clint Barkley finds them, we'll be long gone."

Thirteen

Jo lay quietly for a long time after she heard the cattle rustlers leave. She wondered if Bobby and Flora Mae had gone to sleep. Finally she said, "I think they're gone for good. We'd better get out of here and go tell Uncle Clint."

"Sure," Bobby scoffed. "How we gonna do that?"

"Like the rustlers said, we're not going anywhere." Flora Mae's voice sounded like she had been crying.

"I'm not giving up that easy," Jo said.

"What can we do? They've got us tied real good," Bobby said.

"I've got an idea." Jo began rolling toward Flora Mae. Each time she moved, the rope cut deeper into her wrists. She gritted her teeth against the pain and continued inching her way closer.

"What are you doing?" Bobby asked.

"If we can get lined up right, maybe Flora Mae can reach in my pocket and get my knife."

"Ouch, it hurts too much," Flora Mae said as she tried to move toward Jo.

"I s'pose you'd rather just lie here and wait for the mountain lions," Jo snapped. "I know it hurts but we've got to try to get ourselves out of here. If we wait to be rescued, the rustlers will get away."

Jo continued to struggle to get her pocket where Flora Mae could reach it. Finally, they got lined up, but Jo's pocket wasn't big enough for both of Flora Mae's hands.

"Now what do we do?" Flora Mae leaned back against the rock wall to rest.

"Maybe we can tip my pocket upside down from the outside." Jo struggled to get hold of the bottom of her pocket with her finger tips. "There," she said, "see if you can work the knife on out."

With Flora Mae's prodding, the knife fell out onto the floor of the cave.

"What good did that do?" Flora Mae asked. "It's too dark in here to find it."

With fingers numb from the tight rope around her wrists, Jo searched the floor. Her hand finally bumped into the knife and she was able to pick it up. But when she fumbled to open the blade, she dropped it again.

"It's no use," Flora Mae complained. "We'll never get these ropes untied."

Jo choked back a retort and began groping for the knife again. Finally her fingers bumped into it and she managed to pick it up. After what seemed an eternity, she got the blade open.

In spite of the coolness of the cave, sweat trickled down Jo's face. How could she cut the rope without cutting Flora Mae's wrist? She managed to slip the knife under the rope so she was cutting away from Flora Mae. As she sawed the sharp knife against the hard rope, her fingers began to slip.

"Dear God," she prayed, "help me hang on." Finally, the knife cut through the rope, and Flora Mae's hands were free.

"Now cut my hands free, and I'll do the rest." It seemed to take forever for Flora Mae to saw through the rope.

Once Jo had the use of her hands, it didn't take her long to cut the ropes from her feet. She released the others and groped her way to the mouth of the cave. Bobby and Flora Mae followed.

"How are we going to find our horses in the dark?" Bobby asked.

"The moon will be up soon. You wait here with Flora Mae while I go get the horses."

"Don't get lost, Jo." Flora Mae's voice was still shaky, but Jo was surprised she hadn't completely freaked out on them.

Jo wished she felt as confident as she acted. As the moon cast its eerie light over the mountain, she wasn't sure she could find the horses. Everything looked different in the moonlight. For a moment, she panicked. Then, getting hold of herself, she took a bearing from the rocks above the cave. She knew the horses were down hill, so she started picking her way through the brush and rocks. Once she stumbled and fell full length on the rough ground. Her face and hands stung, but she was able to get up and walk. She stopped every few minutes to listen for the horses. At last she heard a muffled sound like a horse blowing its nose.

"Little Rascal, is that you?" she called.

A nicker greeted her from the aspen grove and she broke into a trot.

"Boy, am I glad to see you," she said as she stroked Little Rascal's neck. Little Rascal nickered again and rubbed his nose on her sleeve. Jo tightened the cinch, untied the horses, and swung into the saddle. With Little Rascal's reins in her left hand and leading Appie and Black Star with her right, she started up the hill toward the cave.

At the cave, Jo dismounted and tightened Black Star's cinch while Bobby tightened Appie's.

"Here's your horse," she said to Flora Mae. "I hope you're not too shook up to ride."

"I'll be all right. Let's get away from this horrible place."

Jo and Little Rascal led the way down the trail at a walk. Jo gave him his head, knowing he could pick the trail better than she in the pale moonlight.

"When we get to the road, I'm going to ride on ahead. Bobby, you stay behind with Flora Mae and see that she gets back to the ranch in one piece."

The bushes cast spooky shadows across the trail. Jo imagined a bobcat or mountain lion behind every bush. She pushed these thoughts from her mind and rode on. What a relief to see the road at last.

"Bobby, get off and hold Appie and Black Star until I get down around the first bend. They might think they're supposed to keep up with Little Rascal." With that she lifted the reins and Little Rascal took off on a run. She let him go at top speed until he was breathing hard, then slowed him to a walk. After that they alternated between a trot and an easy lope.

Lamp light shone from the window of the ranch house when Jo rode into the yard. She couldn't tell what time it was but thought it must be well past bedtime. Aunt Myrtle and Punky came out on the porch. As Jo swung from the saddle, Punky took charge of Little Rascal.

"Jo, are you all right? Where have you been? Where are Bobby and Flora Mae?" Aunt Myrtle gathered Jo in her arms.

"They're coming. Where's Uncle Clint?"

"He's out with all the other ranchers in the valley searching for you."

"I need to talk to him right away."

"Here they come now," Aunt Myrtle said. Jo looked up to see Uncle Clint and several other ranchers ride into the yard. Uncle Clint leaped from his horse and came up the porch steps three at a time.

"Where have you been? We've been combing the whole valley. Just about to start dragging the river." Uncle Clint's voice was gruff, but his hands were gentle as he hugged Jo to him.

"Oh, Uncle Clint, I'm sorry, but we had to find out about the secret cave."

"What secret cave? Where are the others?"

"I'll explain it all later. Right now you've got to catch the rustlers. They're driving the cattle to Red Creek Reservoir. A truck is to meet them there just before daylight."

"You're sure about this?"

"Yes. They had us tied up in the cave. We heard them make all their plans. I'll tell you all about it later, but now you've got to hurry to catch them before they get away. They said they would drive the cattle down Chuck Hollow to Red Creek and follow the creek down to the reservoir."

"How many were there?"

"There were three white men and an Indian at the cave."

"There's probably five or six of them, then. They'd leave one or two men with the herd."

Uncle Clint turned to the men waiting in the yard. "Any of you men who want to ride in a posse, go home and get your gun. Meet me at the town hall in half an hour. I'll ride over there and make a phone call to the sheriff in Duchesne."

Aunt Myrtle went into the house and came back with Uncle Clint's gun belt.

"Thanks, Myrt." He took the gun belt and put it on.

"What are you going to do, Clint?"

"I'll ask the sheriff to get some men together to drive up to Red Creek Reservoir and cut them off from that end. We'll ride down Red Creek and close in behind them. They won't have a chance."

"Be careful."

"Sure." Uncle Clint planted a kiss on Aunt Myrtle's forehead and ran down the steps. He vaulted onto Strawberry and clattered across the bridge.

Fourteen

After Uncle Clint left, Bobby and Flora Mae rode into the yard. Buck Too Tall was with them.

"Where'd you find these strays?" Aunt Myrtle asked.

"Riding up the Farm Creek road. This young lady's plumb tuckered out." Buck swung off his horse and tossed the reins to Bobby. Then, he lifted Flora Mae from the saddle and carried her into the house.

While Aunt Myrtle and Lorna took care of Flora Mae, Jo and Buck went out on the porch. Jo collapsed into the hammock and Buck sat on a bench. Jo felt her muscles begin to relax in the quiet night as moonlight bathed her face and a slight breeze brought the scent of roses. She was starting to drift off when Buck broke the silence.

"You caused quite a stir here in our peaceful valley. Want to tell me about it?"

Jo sat up in the hammock. She started with the day they found the cave and told him all that had happened.

"Why would an Indian be mixed up with rustlers?" Jo asked.

"The rustlers probably promised to pay him for helping them with a cover up."

"He sure had us fooled. We thought the cave really was Chief Tabby's grave. Then, when you said you went to Chief Tabby's burial over by White Rocks, I got suspicious."

Neither spoke for a time, then Jo said, "What about the other Indians, the ones that don't do bad things like rustle cattle? Not many of them have good ranches like you do. Uncle Clint says they'd rather go hunting and fishing. Does that mean they're lazy?"

"There's more to it than laziness. Hunting and fishing was our way of life before white men came." In the moonlight, Jo saw that sad, far away look come into his eyes again.

"What the white men did to your people was awful. Are you still mad at them?"

"No, Jo. Anger spreads like a festering sore in a man's soul. I had to find a way to get rid of it."

"What did you do?"

"My father was Chief Tabby's friend. Like the good chief, he could see the only way to survive was to get along with the white men and learn from them. He told me to go to the white men's school. So I went to school here on the reservation through eighth grade. Then I went away to a mission school where I learned about Jesus. Jesus taught me how to forgive.

"I'm glad I still have my Ute language. I'm proud of my Ute heritage, but I've let go of the past with its grudges. Jesus has given me a love for white men. Your Uncle Clint is my best friend."

Jo felt a tightening in her stomach and thought of Grandpa. She could hear him say, "Flora Mae needs you to forgive her. Are you big enough for that?"

After Buck left, everyone went to bed, but Jo didn't get much sleep. Toward morning she drifted off and slept until after sunup. Uncle Clint and Rod rode in about noon.

"The sheriff and his men caught the rustlers," Uncle Clint said as the family ate lunch. "We drove the cattle back. As soon as I get a bite to eat and some sleep, I want a report from you kids."

That evening, Jo told about their adventure on the mountain.

"That was a tomfool thing to do," Uncle Clint blustered. "You could have got yourselves killed. Still, I have to say you sure got grit. Why didn't you tell us what you suspected?"

"We promised the Indian we wouldn't tell anyone about the secret cave. We couldn't break our promise, and you said it wasn't right to accuse anyone unless you had evidence."

"Jo, you're something else. Next time you go looking for evidence on suspected criminals call in some adult help."

The next few days everyone was busy getting ready for the cattle drive. Uncle Clint arranged for Bucky to come over and milk the cows and feed the chickens while they were gone.

"We need all our crew on the cattle drive," he explained. "All you cowpokes who are going to ride will have to be up early. We start the herd up the road at daybreak. Myrt will drive the truck up later in the day with the food and camping gear and set up camp for us on the west fork of the Duchesne River."

"Aunt Myrtle, may I come with you and help set up camp?" Flora Mae asked. "After all I've been through, I don't think I'm ready for that long a ride."

"Sounds good to me," Aunt Myrtle said. "Then Lorna can have her horse to help drive the cattle."

Everyone was up before first light the next morning to feed and saddle the horses. The morning was clear and a light frost covered the ground. Jo's numb fingers fumbled with the saddle leather. The cold seeped through her warm jacket.

After a breakfast of Aunt Myrtle's flapjacks, Jo and Bobby were ready. This was the adventure they'd been waiting for. Before the sun peeked over Big Mountain, Uncle Clint gave the word to move them out.

"Jo, you ride ahead," Uncle Clint said. "Cross the creek at the ford and keep the cattle from going on up the road."

Jo urged Little Rascal to a gallop and rode out around the milling, bawling herd. Little Rascal splashed across the creek. He wasn't about to stand quietly and wait. Jo moved him in circles.

"Easy, boy." She patted him on the neck. "I'm just as eager to get going as you, but we gotta be patient."

The bawling grew louder and one cow splashed across the creek followed by a calf. She took one look at the quirt Jo was twirling and headed down the road. Others followed. One little mixed-up calf started up the road but Little Rascal whipped after him like a frog's tongue after a fly.

"Take them slow and easy," Uncle Clint said. "Bobby, you ride up alongside the herd. Appie'll keep those calves out of the willows."

One determined cow darted back toward the ranch. Jo watched spellbound as Rod and Roanie worked to get her back in the herd. It was like Roanie could read her mind. If she darted one way, Roanie was one jump ahead of her. Just as quickly, they darted back the other way. Jo was so absorbed in watching Roanie, she didn't notice a calf turn back from the herd. Little Rascal noticed, and Jo almost lost her seat as he went after the calf.

"You're not at a rodeo, Jo." Uncle Clint laughed. "You better pay attention to your own horse."

As they approached Tabiona, Uncle Clint sent Jo, Punky, and Lorna on ahead.

"You've got to keep them from going on down the road past Tabiona or across the bridge up Tabby Mountain."

When they came to the main road, the herd tried to split three ways. It took some hard riding to get them all headed in the right direction. They had settled down and were moving along well when a car came up the road from behind.

"Here comes trouble," Rod shouted. "That's an out-of-state license." He tried to ride ahead to split the herd and let the car through, but the car kept coming too fast. The driver honked his horn and stuck his head out the window.

"Get those stupid cows out of my way," he shouted.

Jo watched in anger as cows and calves scattered into the brush along the river and the car sped on up the road. One cow, separated from her calf, came back down the road toward Jo and Little Rascal. Jo swung her quirt at her as Little Rascal dodged back and forth, jump for jump with the cow. Uncle Clint and the others rounded up cows and calves out of the willows along the river. They finally got them headed back up the road.

"Don't try to push them," Uncle Clint said. "We'll just hold them here for a little while and give the cows a chance to find their calves. You kids can get off and walk a little to get warmed up."

Jo swung from the saddle, glad for the chance to get the circulation going. Her fingers were numb and her toes tingled.

When they started pushing the herd on up the road, one little calf straggled behind.

"Guess you're going to have to piggy back that one, Lorna," Uncle Clint said. "He's too young to keep up."

Lorna eased herself over the back of the saddle to ride on Black Star's rump. Rod lifted the calf and laid it across the saddle. The mother cow walked beside Black Star, mooing softly to her calf. They moved along without any trouble for a while. Rod fished his harmonica out of his shirt pocket and played some tunes.

"Here comes more trouble," Jo said as a car came up from behind.

"This won't be bad; that's a neighbor." Rod put the harmonica back in his pocket and rode ahead to split the herd. The neighbor waved and drove slowly through without scattering the cattle.

The sun beat down. Dust hung in the air and in Jo's nose, eyes, and ears. She took off her jacket and tied it behind the saddle.

"I'm starved," Bobby said as he rode up alongside of Jo.

"Tighten your belt. We should get the word soon to eat our lunch."

"What's this, mutiny in the ranks?" Uncle Clint rode up beside them.

"No, just a kid who always has an empty leg." Jo laughed.

"Another half hour up the trail we should come to a good place to water the herd and let them shade up for a little while. Then we'll pull out our sandwiches."

After lunch and a short rest they got the herd moving again. Things went well until late afternoon when they came to the West Fork of the Duchesne River. Here they had to push the cattle across the river just above the bridge. It was boggy by the river. Little Rascal sank in half way up to his knees. Riding him was like riding a bucking horse. Jo thought of Flora Mae. It was a good thing she had chosen to ride in the truck with Aunt Myrtle.

A couple of miles beyond the ford, the trail left the river and went up Wolf Creek.

"We'll push them as far as Blue Lake," Uncle Clint said. "By that time Myrt will have camp set up for us on the West Fork. We'll spend the night there. That way we can be sure none of the cattle drift back down before they get settled on their summer range."

After supper they sat around the campfire reliving the events of the day.

"Did you bring my guitar, Ma?" Rod asked.

"It's in the truck. Cow camp wouldn't be complete without some of your songs."

They sang cowboy songs for a while. Then Rod said, "Now we'll sing 'Billy Boy,' and you can make up verses."

Jo grinned at Flora Mae and sang, "Can she milk a Jersey cow, Billy Boy, Billy Boy? Can she milk a Jersey cow, charming Billy? She can milk a Jersey Cow, quick as a cat can say meow. She's a young thing and cannot leave her mother."

Punky took it up next: "Can she ride a bucking horse, Billy Boy, Billy Boy? Can she ride a bucking horse, charming Billy? She can ride a bucking horse, but she may fall off of course. She's a young thing and cannot leave her mother." Jo made a face at Punky and everyone laughed until the tears ran down their cheeks.

"We're all so tired we're silly," Aunt Myrtle said, wiping her eyes with her handkerchief. "You cowpokes better hit your bedrolls. You've still got to ride all the way home tomorrow."

Jo pulled off her boots and crawled in between her blankets. She lay looking up at the stars. At last she had helped with a real cattle drive. It had been a perfect day. Why did she still have this unsettled feeling in her stomach? She could hear Buck saying, "Jesus taught me how to forgive. I'm proud of my Ute heritage, but I've let go of the past with its old grudges."

Somehow she had to let go of the past. She must tell Flora Mae that she no longer nursed a grudge against her. Jo went to sleep with Grandpa's words drifting through her mind: "Are you big enough for that?"

Fifteen

"How are you feeling, Flora Mae?" Jo asked as they broke camp the next morning.

"I'm okay."

"Wanna ride with us on the way back?"

"I'd like to if it's all right with Lorna. I'll go ask her."

Lorna agreed to ride home in the truck and let Flora Mae ride Black Star.

"We'll let the others ride on ahead if they're in a hurry," Jo said. "I'd like to take time to enjoy the beautiful morning."

The sun was already warm. Wild flowers brightened the roadside and bird songs filled the air. Jo thought this would be a good time to talk to Flora Mae. They put their horses on a slow lope for a little way, then slowed them to a walk.

"I saw how you helped Aunt Myrtle around camp last night and this morning," Jo said. "You've really learned to make yourself useful."

"It's good to feel useful. I used to think it was fun to have everyone wait on me. You've taught me a lot, Jo."

"I've been pretty hard on you. Buck told me about his people who can't let go of the past. He said they still nurse a grudge against the white men. I'm afraid I've never really forgiven you about Marybel."

"Does it still hurt that much, Jo?"

"Yes, but I don't want to hang on to the past. I really do want us to be friends."

"We've got the rest of the summer to work at it." Flora Mae smiled, and Jo felt the warmth of that smile. Maybe she could learn to like Flora Mae.

That evening Buck Too Tall and his family came over to Uncle Clint's. Bucky carried a paper bag. They all sat out on the porch and visited.

"I hear you're leaving us in the morning," Buck said.

"Yeah. Uncle Charlie's coming tonight so we can leave first thing tomorrow morning."

"It's not going to be the same around here without you kids. We'll remember you as the kids who caught the rustlers."

"Who got caught by the rustlers is more like it," Rod said.

"I'll remember Jo as the one who got bucked off Little Rascal." Punky ducked as Jo threw her shoe at him.

"We've been a lot of trouble for you, Aunt Myrtle," Flora Mae said.

"Lands, no. It's been good to have you."

"All of you were a real help on the cattle drive." Uncle Clint got that twinkle in his eye that reminded Jo of Dad. "Next time just leave the detective work to someone else."

"We brought a little something for you to remember us by. Bucky, hand me that bag." Buck reached in the bag and pulled out a beaded necklace. "This is for you, Flora Mae."

"Oh, it's gorgeous! Thank you." Flora Mae placed the necklace around her neck.

"And for Bobby, a pair of moccasins."

"Gee, thanks." Bobby slipped his feet into the beaded buckskin moccasins.

"And for the cowgirl who's going to own a ranch some day and train her own horses, a pair of gauntlet gloves."

Jo was speechless as she accepted the gloves of soft buckskin. The gauntlets, covered with fine beadwork, reached half way to her elbows.

When she could speak, she turned to Mrs. Too Tall. "Did you make these?"

Mrs. Too Tall nodded shyly. Jo grasped both her hands and squeezed them. Then she threw herself into Buck's arms.

"Oh, Buck," she said, with tears in her eyes. "Thank you. I'll treasure these forever. And thank you for all you've taught me about horses and about your people."

Flora Mae was already in bed when Jo went upstairs later that evening. As she laid the gauntlet gloves on the dresser, she ran her fingers over the bead work. She could hardly believe these beautiful buckskin gloves were really hers.

Lorna's old boots leaned against each other near the dresser. Jo picked them up and carried them down to the hall closet.

"What are you doing, Jo?" Aunt Myrtle asked.

"I'm returning Lorna's boots."

"You may have them."

"Oh, Aunt Myrtle, thank you. I've always wanted a pair of cowboy boots." She gave Aunt Myrtle a hug, then floated up the stairs hugging the boots to her.

Jo snuggled in bed and gazed at the night sky. The stars looked so close she could almost reach up and touch one. She lay a long time thinking of all that had happened at the ranch. She could hardly wait to tell Grandpa.

"Flora Mae, you asleep?" she whispered.

"No. Too excited."

"Know what? I think we're friends already."